The Glass Boy

By
H.C. Tharsing

For Walter K. Smith, who asked me to tell him a story

Acknowledgements

I thank all my friends and family for supporting me and this project over the years it has taken to bring this book to press. First among these, I thank my sisters, "the Three Graces": Penny Taylor, Pat Hardebeck, and Marianne Willard. Your generosity has overwhelmed me, giving as you have of your financial and intellectual resources as well as blessing me with your sustaining love for your little brother.

Second, I thank all the friends and family members who, like my sisters, read drafts or listened to readings and provided insight, encouragement, and direction: Gerald Halpern, Chuck Forester, Bob Sass, Jeff Leiphart, Mike Discepola, John Reese, Ronald Aguilera, Auntie Jeanie, and especially Ruth and Walt Smith. My dear friend Pat Holt, too, deserves special mention for fearlessly wading through the entire manuscript in an earlier form and for making comments that both encouraged and challenged me. All of these friends and family members kept me going at times when I might easily have let my doubts deter me from completing the book.

Finally, I want to thank Matthew Martinez, who more than anyone else believed in the glass boy and in me. He read and listened to drafts and revisions of the entire book, more than once, and patiently pointed out strengths and weaknesses. He has also been an advocate for and promoter of the project with others who have themselves become readers and supporters. I hope you know, Matthew, how much you have done for me, in this instance as in countless others in our life together.

Contents

Introduction   **1**

PART ONE

One   **5**

The glass boy's early life; Shipwrecked men; Leaving home

Two   **25**

Gus's philosophy (1); Two day's journey; The fire

Three   **35**

Gus's philosophy (2); Nick's philosophy; The City

PART TWO

Four   **47**

Billy takes charge; Going to Johnnie's; The clock shop

Five   **75**

Billy calls Louis; Upstairs at Johnnie's; The Tower; Marty's resentment

Six   **89**

Leaving Johnnie's; Eavesdropping; A gunfight; Joe's ride; Nick's garden apartment

PART THREE

Seven   **114**

*Joe and Siria; Gus and the boy; Siria consults Verre;
Marty conspires with Joe*

Eight   **129**

Billy's dream; Nick joins the conspiracy

Nine   **143**

*Siria, Verre, and Pappas in the church; Johnnie finds
his way upstairs*

PART FOUR

Ten   **166**

*Johnnie joins the conspiracy; Billy dictates to Louis;
Julie arrives; Billy joins Gus and the boy*

Eleven   **192**

*Billy takes the boy to chapel; The press conference;
Julie's interview; Siria bundled off*

Twelve   **210**

The earthquake; Fire at the Parish House

PART FIVE

Thirteen   **228**

*A makeshift hospital; Billy injured; "The Lord giveth
. . . "*

Fourteen   **244**

*Nick's goodbye; Pappas leaves the chapel; Marty
observes the people of The City*

Fifteen   **257**

*Under Chinatown; Gus's voyage; The cabin; The
Chapel; The mountain; The beach*

Introduction

In preparing this new edition of the text for publication, it has been the editor's intention to sort through all of the evidence that survives from the period. These sources consist for the most part of the public record, such as published books, articles, and video footage, but I have also included material from unpublished personal notes, emails, letters, and journal entries. The object has been to render a single, coherent, chronological narrative of whatever events can be corroborated by more than one source.

There is one exception to this standard, and that pertains to those portions of the story that concern events which were related to others by the glass boy himself. I wish to be clear in stating that only these scenes are based on hearsay: Otherwise, all events can be found in at least two sources. For the most part, these portions of the narrative cover the boy's life with his mother, prior to his first encounter with human beings.

We know nothing of the origins, possible parentage, or even the age of the mother of the glass boy. Nor do we know her name.[1]

---

[1] Like many primitive people, the glass boy refused to utter his own name or that of any of his family

We do know that the boy described his mother as having always lived on the little bay where he grew up, and that he called her "Guardian of the Bay," saying that it was her constant practice "to do whatever she could to slow the sea's relentless gnawing at the land."

Some writers, suggesting that the mother of the glass boy was a Nereid, closely related to Psamatheia,[2] have woven fanciful tales about her based on the Greek myth. Other scholars have insisted that what little we know about the mother identifies her with the "shape-shifters" of Native American lore. At times she was anthropoid in form, but she was also capable of "disintegrating" and becoming a loose mass of sand that moved continually in the winds and the waves. On this point, the editor believes both the Nativists and the Psamatheists have some credibility, because Psamatheia is said to have been the daughter of Proteus.

H. C. Tharsing
Oakland, California

---

members.

[2] Aaron J. Atsma, PSAMATHE, Theoi Project, 2000-2008,

http://www.theoi.com/Pontios/NereisPsamathe.html (10/2009)

PART ONE

*For the LORD God formed man of the dust
of the ground, and breathed into his nostrils
the breath of life . . .*
[Genesis 2:7]

One

There once lived a boy who was made of glass.

His mother was made of sand.

He knew nothing of his father.

The glass boy looked almost the same as any other boy you might know. He was not transparent, like a window pane, nor did he look smooth and clear like a crystal sculpture such as the exquisite Lalique might have made. His body, in its shape and size, in its flexibility, and in its motions, were like those of a human boy of about the same age.

But in spite of these similarities, the moment you first saw him, you knew that you were in the presence of someone -- or something -- prodigious, unimaginable, even inexplicable. You had to believe the unbelievable because it was what you saw: a boy who was made out of glass.

How was he different? Consider how your flesh looks uniformly colored and fairly dull, not shiny or sparkling. His flesh, on the other hand, reflected and refracted light, like a highly polished crystal ball, on the surface of which, if you focus your eyes on the surface, you see yourself and the world around you reflected, but inside which, if you focus your eyes on its interior, you see shapes of light broken into the spectrum of colors and lines and planes defined by the structure of the crystal itself.

You might say that the boy of glass looked solid and permanent where we look soft and vulnerable. You got the feeling that his body was made of something that might melt or shatter but would not, like our bodies, burn or rot. And at times the light seemed actually to enter into him and to shine back from within.

This boy of glass lived with his mother beside the sea. Their home was on a small, tightly curved bay, surrounded by cliffs that rose to a height of two hundred feet, like impenetrable walls of stone. Where, precisely, that bay was, we cannot say. But it was at the edge of our world, where the continent falls into the sea. The thunder of the waves always sounded there. The sound was as familiar to the boy as his own heartbeat, so that over the years he became unaware of it, just as you are unaware of the sound of your own heartbeat or the sound your breathing.

The glass boy's mother said that the sound of the waves was the sound of life out there, in the world. Here, in their little home by the sea, in a cave at the base of the cliffs, they were safe. Out there, in the world, life came down like waves, smashing everything to bits, over and over and over again.

A boy such as he, a boy of glass, could not expect to survive the waves. It was here, at home, that he belonged.

The boy's mother had always lived there, guardian of the little bay, doing what she could to slow the sea's relentless gnawing at the land. Where the roots of a young oak or manzanita had been exposed by the erosion of the cliffs, she would shore it up, holding soil and rock in place, protecting life. So too she hid the clams from the cormorants and gulls, and she sheltered even the tiny sand flies when the harsh winds blew. While she passed her days tending to these things, the glass boy spent the bulk of his time swimming, rock-climbing, or exploring the tide pools that teemed with forms of life that hinted at earlier and other creation.

Being a child, the glass boy obeyed his mother's command not to wander beyond the confines of their bay, and he did so without question. He did not think of exploring what might lie above and beyond the cliffs. Instead he spent most of his waking hours playing in the water, an element which relieved him, at least partially, of the burden of his own weight.

For even though the glass boy's body looked much like the body of an ordinary boy, and even though he moved through the world in much the same way that human beings move, he did so with much greater difficulty, requiring much greater strength, than an ordinary boy. Being made of glass meant being built out of silicon, whereas we humans are built out of carbon. And the silicon in his tissues weighed over twice what the carbon in our tissues does.[1] This additional weight led to the development of extraordinary strength in his limbs, and it necessitated that he metabolize tremendous amounts of energy.

So because of the relative difficulty he experienced in moving, the buoyancy of the ocean's salt water in which he swam gave the glass boy a sense of liberation even greater than that which it gives to human beings. So enthusiastic was he about being in the water, that by the time the glass boy reached the age of 18 months, he had already learned not just to keep afloat and not drown, but in fact to swoop and dive and slide through the waves

---

[1] The atomic weight of silicon is 28; that of carbon is 12.

like a bird in flight. He felt most alive, most free, in the water.

It was in the water too that he found the foods most nourishing to him. The glass boy derived a great deal of energy by eating foods rich in silicon, such as horsetail and other grasses; diatoms that were abundant in the water of the bay; and animals having a lot of cartilage, such as shark. And he had one capability that we cannot begin to match: the boy who was made of glass could draw energy directly from sunlight, just as the silicon wafers at the heart of photovoltaic cells transform the energy of light into energy of another form.

As the years passed, the glass boy grew close to manhood still inexperienced in the ways of the world. He had seen nothing of the great world outside his mother's little bay, except for the sight of the ships far out at sea, passing intermittently, moving at a moderate, deliberate pace, steady with a weight that puzzled him, a weight beyond reason considering their tiny size. He was fascinated by them as they moved majestically through the endless waves. The boy could not understand how they passed in that way, and in his dreams he would reach for the tiny ships, just as, when he looked up into the open sky on nights that came dark and clear, he wanted to reach for the stars that sparkled with such brilliance when the night.

At the end of each day, when the sun began to set, the glass boy would return to the cave in which he and his mother made their home. Nestled under the cliff-face, at the northern end of the bay, this small, natural shelter held only a table, two chairs, two beds, a cupboard and some shelves. There the boy who was made of glass would wait for his mother.

When she came to him, the sand lying just outside the threshold of the cave would begin to pile itself up like the sand in the lower half of an hourglass, but piling up from below rather than falling from above. The pile would grow quickly, its shape variously contracting into a waist and expanding into a torso and limbs. At last her head would rise from her shoulders, her face taking shape around her smile. And in the earliest light of dawn, she would do the same in reverse, her body slowly collapsing into itself, like the sand in the upper half of an hourglass, simultaneously flowing out over the ground and under the water.

It was at night that his mother taught the glass boy what she knew about the world encompassed by the curved wall of rock surrounding their bay. The boy was a good student, listening dutifully and committing everything to memory in the moment he heard it. He did not have to be told anything twice but seemed to have etched each word or image into his silicon brain at once.

The boy listened with a special delight when, as he lay in bed at the end of his nightly lessons, she would tell him stories of the larger world that lay beyond their ken. The stories were usually myths concerning the great forces that shape the world and the lives of all the creatures in it. Occasionally she would speak of some extraordinary event involving one or more of the creatures who inhabited their bay, something she had witnessed herself. None of her stories, however, involved her as a participant. Every night, while she would tell the glass boy these stories, her soft voice rising and falling like the rush and withdrawal of the waves breaking in the darkness outside their cave, the glass boy's eyelids would grow heavy, and he would feel the energy flowing out of his limbs, as he sank into sleep.

The boy seems not to have asked his mother about her early life, but then few children do. A child sees his parent as a permanent fixture, a stronghold to which he or she can cling amid the swirl of his or her own experiences. It is only when we reach adulthood that we realize that we are the age our parents were when they were living the stories that we have so often heard from them, stories that seem to us as children to emerge from the dimness of an impossibly far gone past. It is only then that we begin to perceive our parents not only as adults but as adults who were once children, as adults who have their lives in their time, as we have ours in ours. Only then do we begin to have our life, as we then experience it.

If we are fortunate, we seize the opportunity of that moment to ask our parents about their lives. But few of us are lucky in that way, and most of us go on knowing nothing more about our parents' youths than what is contained in the handful of stories that are told and retold whenever the family gathers, stories concerning a few momentous, or particularly comic, events, such as the beginnings of a romance that became a marriage, a family, us. Rare is the child who thinks to ask his parents about their history in the days before his own began.

*

One night, the boy awoke to a sound he had never heard before, a small sound full of tension, a hoarse sound.

As he awakened, the boy realized that the sound was piercing the much louder blasts of thunder and the heavy pounding of the waves of a monstrous storm. He looked quickly around the cave. His mother was gone.

The boy's first memory, his oldest memory, returned to him, as it did during every storm, with utter clarity even though he could not have been more than three or four years old at the time.

He remembered being truly terrified for the first time in his life, as his mother woke him in the night, the rising of the wind outside foretelling a storm to come. The wind was not yet strong enough to have awakened him, and he was not yet old enough to know what terror it could -- and, in fact, would -- hold as the night wore on.

What frightened him was his mother. She leaned over his bed, shaking him by the shoulders, trembling and sweaty, her hair flying up around her head, blown by gusts of wind that were finding their way deep inside their cave.

His mother saw the fear in his eyes, and for a few minutes managed to calm herself. Pulling the glass boy close, she murmured "Shhhh, shhhh," in his ear, holding his head against her cheek and rocking him as he sat up in his bed.

"Don't worry, my child. You are safe here," she said. "You will be safe, I swear to you. But now I must leave you alone. No matter what happens, you must not leave this cave: no matter what happens."

Then she pulled away from him and, holding his head between her hands, peered into his mirror-like face. "Do you understand me, child?" she asked softly, with the look that terrified the boy coming back into her eyes.

Shaking, the boy answered, "Yes."

Then she let go of him, and, as he fell back on his bed, her eyes went vacant, as if she were pulled from him by a sound that she alone could hear. She rose and turned away. She walked into the darkness and was gone.

At the end of that first terrible storm of his childhood, as the dawn began to show him the world again, the boy saw that his mother had returned. She lay exhausted on the floor, just inside the cave, sleeping. Toward the end of the morning, when she at last awoke, the boy asked her what had happened and where she had gone.

"The storm came," she said.

She would say no more.

She did not tell him, on that day or at any time since, where she went when the storms came. Over the years, whenever the great storms hit, she disappeared. The boy believed that she battled the storms to save him. He imagined that she threw herself into the fists of the storm and by doing so somehow shielded their home.

Now again alone, in this other storm, he listened to the new, thin sound he heard within the chaos outside. As he did, the boy slowly realized that the sound was not mere sound. It compelled him to listen more closely. He strained to hear it in the din. It called him out of himself, his mind racing into the turbulent darkness outside. Then the boy knew what the sound was: it was speech.

The boy felt sick. No voice but his mother's had ever spoken in his ears. Now a strange squawking formed words. With the passage of but a few minutes, he began to be able to discern several disparate voices in the storm, falling over each other, crying out to one another.

"Help!"

"God!"

"Joe! Gus! Nick!"

"Help me!"

Terrified, the boy held himself tight, not daring to go to the mouth of the cave. Still, woven in the thunderous storm, the thin strands of speech pouring in seemed to fill the cave. Someone was crying out, at the end of hope. They needed help. He must go.

So the boy who was made of glass made his way cautiously to the entrance of the cave and beheld a storm for the first time. The land in front of the cave had disappeared. Waves broke at the threshold. His eyes burned in the slashing wind laden with salt. And as the storm robbed him of sight, his hearing became more acute, searching the chaos of the storm, its rage, for those desperate, small voices within it.

The boy took a step forward, into the water, and stood for a moment, in awe, his legs anchored in the swirling water. He understood his mother's warnings, her fear for him. But now he knew that she had been wrong. He stood in the wild dark and did not break. The hard, cold waves broke over him.

They did not harm him. He was himself unbroken.

The glass boy smiled with pride. He knew that he must do this, that he was right to do this. He felt that his mother, wherever she might be in this pounding fury, must be supporting him.

He waded out into the surf, the cold water sliding over his limbs and torso without effect, as he gathered in his arms first one of the creatures and then another, bringing them one by one up onto the thin marge of dry land that remained at the base of the cliffs. There he lay them down. Once all five of them were out of danger, the glass boy slipped away to watch them from a distance. He did not stay in their company but was gone before they could look round and see where they were.

It took some time before the sailors regained the strength to talk, and even when they could, each found himself with nothing to say, each feeling oddly uncomfortable, aware of some nebulous idea that frightened them. All five of them were together, but each could have sworn that there had been six of them there on the sand, as the storm had begun to fade.

Hollowing a shallow pit in the sand, they

gathered driftwood and shattered bits of their broken boat, piling it all next to the pit. They selected the driest pieces and arranged them carefully in the pit. Then one of them drew a small box from his pocket, and they huddled close together, bending over the pile they had made.

The boy watched them from the darkness where he sat, keeping watch also for his mother's return.

Where was his mother? The storm had passed, and yet she had not returned. And what could these sea-creatures be? They were slippery like fish, but more seal than fish. They squawked like birds, but their squawking was not gibberish but words, expressions, speech.

As the boy watched them, they conjured in their midst something like the sun, but small and shuddering, shaking, bowing to the wind, yet leaping back to full form in the breaks between gusts, subtle and changing and staying alive in the midst of everything. The creatures gathered even closer round it in a tight circle, protecting it. Yet they seemed to feel protected by it, too, nurturing it and clinging to it.

The men huddled together, the boy made of

glass at a little distance from them, through the last hour of the night, until it began to mingle with dawn. They did not speak. After their struggle against the water, the men wanted only to inhale the peace, the relief, of their own stillness. Beside them, the sea, though retreating, raged on.

The men passed in and out of sleep during that hour. Waking, they sometimes gazed into the shadows and saw the firelight glinting off of the boy's face. Then they turned their eyes back to the fire and dozed again. The hopes and fears that flickered in the firelight were reflected in the boy, and these hopes and fears wove themselves together into stories that the men dreamed that they had heard.

*

Anyone who has ever watched out a night knows that the dawn's dim lifting comes so slowly that we miss its start. All at once we realize that we are already seeing again the world and that we have been holding it in sight for some time, unaware. We are blind to the beginning of day.

So it was for the glass boy, who suddenly realized that day had come, that his mother must be home, and that he, who had promised never to leave during a storm, was not where he should be. He rose swiftly from his place near the circle of men and ran down the shoreline into the dark and the heavy mist, toward the cliffs, which still stood in the shadow of night.

The boy of glass ran to the threshold of the cave and stopped short. He balanced on the balls of his feet and drew a breath. He peered into the darkness inside.

His mother was not, as he had expected, prostrate on the floor, asleep, as she had been on the morning after the first storm and after every storm since. Instead, she sat at their small table, head fallen on her folded arms, weeping. The boy's shoulders drooped, and he bowed his head as he came through the door.

She did not raise her head even to look at him. She drew a breath and spoke into her folded arms.

"I have been afraid," she said. "So afraid."

"Don't be, Mama," said the boy. "I'm fine. Look."

Her head rose from her arms, but she did not turn to look at him. She showed him the back of her head as she spoke.

"I saw you with them." She paused and took another breath. "I have seen them before."

Then the boy's mother turned to look at the boy. As in that long-ago night of the first storm the boy remembered, her hair was wild and her eyes vacant.

"Your father," she said, her tense voice becoming a low rumble. "Your father came here with men like those. He was among them."

Again her throat stopped her voice. "The next day they were gone," she said.

She had risen from the table and drawn quite close to her boy of glass all the time she was speaking, and now she threw her arms around him and held him close. She rested her head gently against his temple, and her tears ran down his cheek and into his mouth. He tasted salt on his tongue.

When she had calmed, she spoke flatly into his shoulder. "He left with them, and now you will leave with them." His ear burned and the nape of his neck shivered under her breath.

"I won't!" he said as he pulled away from her

21

to look into her eyes. He knew that he lied in the instant he heard the words come from his mouth. He saw in his mother's eyes that she knew it too.

His mother turned her back on him and slowly shuffled toward the table. When she reached it, she slumped again in her chair. The boy stood in the middle of the cave, momentarily at a loss. He felt the distance from where he stood to the table at which she sat go cold.

Still the glass boy's thoughts ran back to his own hopes, as young minds are meant to do. If his father lived among men, and if he could go with these men to whatever place was their home, he might find his father.

He looked again at his mother. He did not know whether he had the courage to disappoint her. He was sure that he would return, and he might return bringing his father. But then the glass boy felt a chill come over him again. He looked outside to see the bright, cold daylight beginning to fill the world between the sea and the foot of the cliffs.

The boy of glass knew that he had to run out into that light and search, however far it might take, to find his father. "I'm sorry, so sorry," he said.

As he turned to go, his mother said "Wait." With her back still turned to him, she rose from the table to go to the cupboard and take down some dried fish, dried kelp, and a jar of berries which he had gathered on the cliffs the previous autumn and which she had put up for winter. They both knew that winter had come.

She put these things and some others into a bag, and she held it out to her son. Taking it from her hand, he put his arms around her and kissed her forehead and held her close for a long moment. Then he watched himself from somewhere overhead as he slowly slipped from her embrace.

The glass boy took his mother's gift over his shoulder and walked down the shifting line of the water's edge, where the continent falls into the wet abyss from which we come. He began to hurry and was soon striding proudly along the arcing line of the stone walls that were the cliffs.

Overhead, gulls, reeling, swooped down to tear at the many kinds of flesh that lay tangled in the wreckage that had been tossed up by the storm. Vultures, too, and crows fed there.

In the distance, the boy could see the men preparing to set off, and he broke into a run, hurrying to join them.

Two

Gus

"It was a difficult journey home. We had a hard enough time getting to the top of the cliffs and onto the headlands. Then we had another day and a half of hiking to reach The City. But I think that's not the only reason none of us has gone back there, to that beach, again. You see, I'm not sure that I could ever find that beach again, and I don't think anyone else could, either.

"And I don't mean just because after a few years you might forget some turn or other that you had to take along the way. I know that this will not make sense to you, but I'm not sure that the beach continued to exist after we left it. I just can't imagine how the ground on which I am standing now could be connected to that beach. It just was not part of the same world.

"I keep thinking about that hike back home. I remember that the farther inland we got, the roar of the surf faded, and I began to hear a faint, jangling sound. I found out later that it was the glass boy's voice, but at first I couldn't figure out where it was coming from. It reminded me of a small glass wind chime that my mother once bought me in Chinatown made of little rectangles of milky-white glass decorated with red and green Chinese characters and a shiny gold chord with a tassel hanging from the bottom. I hadn't thought about it in years, and I got all sentimental. I

missed my mother.

"When I woke up at dawn on the beach, he wasn't there, and I wasn't sure whether he had been real or not. I had felt him grab me in the water, I know that I had, and I know that I had seen his face as he carried me up onto the beach. But I'll bet that if you ask the other guys, none of them really believed what we all seemed to remember.

"But then he came running back to us. We were preparing to head out to the point at the south end of the bay. We were standing there, holding bundles of things that we had salvaged: some tools, a few large pieces of sailcloth, a bucket, some rope. As he got close to us, he stopped running and approached us slowly, as though we were animals that he was afraid of scaring away. He sat down in the sand and opened the sack he had been carrying over his shoulder, showing us the food that he had brought to us. We sat down and ate with him. None of us spoke a word.

"After we ate, the glass boy rose first. He stood up and gathered his things quickly. While we were still shouldering our own, he started off, walking really fast toward the cliffs. Before we could really figure out what he was doing, we were all following him.

"It looked as if he were going to walk right into that wall of rock, and then, with the sunlight so bright that morning that your eyes hurt, he all of a sudden disappeared completely. He had hit a wall of shadow,

not rock, but it looked like he had walked right into the face of the cliff.

"When we followed him, the shadows seemed as bitterly cold as the night before. As my eyes adjusted, I saw the glass boy as a dimly gleaming figure constantly retreating before us. When he reached the base of the cliff, he scampered up the first twenty yards without pausing. Then I began to see cracks along the cliff face revealed by his climbing, and I began to see that some were big enough to provide a foothold. Higher up, the cracks became ledges wide enough to walk, and finally a path.

"Then, for the first time since he had started walking away from us on the beach, the glass boy turned to face us. He looked down at us, and then Nick, the youngest of us, proceeded to put his foot first on one crack in the wall, then on another, confidently. Captain Ferris went next, studying Nick's moves and repeating them slowly and deliberately so that the rest of us could follow as well. It took the whole day to climb that cliff, but we made it. By sunset we were standing atop the headlands and looking down at the sea.

"At the top of the cliff, we found ourselves standing on a slightly rolling grassland that stretched toward a range of mountains in the east. We made camp that night there on the empty field. We used pieces of canvas that we had for ground cloths and blankets. But we were unable to rig any kind of tents because we

27

had no poles and there was no standing wood to cut at all.

"No wood also meant no fire. So we bundled against the cold as best we could. We ate bits of cold meat and bread from the boy's supply. And despite the cold and hunger, we slept soundly, exhausted.

"On the second day, we set out across the grasslands toward the mountains. As the day wore on and we got closer, we started up into foothills, where the incessant winds had bent and twisted the stubbly pines into bizarre shapes. They seemed like alien creatures who held themselves stock-still when we looked at them, their limbs contorted in impossible positions, like dancers photographed in mid-flight. As we made our way to the top of the slope, we saw that on the other side, where they were sheltered from the winds, the same trees grew straight and tall. With them at hand, we had everything we needed to pitch proper tents and to build a fire.

"But the boy didn't stop. He continued to march forward as though neither the walking nor the sun's heat had made him feel any need of rest. We trudged on wearily behind him, muttering about our thirst, about our hunger, about our aching feet, and saying how pleasant the shade felt, how we longed to rest. Still he didn't let up his pace at all.

"We hiked on through the ferns and lilacs, the rustling oak and huckleberry and pines. We saw great flocks of birds, many large enough to provide considerable meat, and we caught glimpses of deer and small game. Both Joe and Marty wondered aloud why the boy was leading us so deep into the forest, and some suspicion began to arise. Was this creature as benign as we had thought? Or was he leading us into a trap?

"For myself, I kept feeling that this boy was not leading us at all, at least not intentionally. He seemed to be walking forward as though he were alone, as though we did not exist for him. I thought it more true to say that we followed him than to say that he led us.

"By late afternoon, we reached a long and narrow bay, more of an inlet, really, that separated the grasslands and forest we had traversed from the mountains ahead of us, three or four miles inland. Once again we wanted to make camp immediately, but the boy turned instead and followed the water's edge south toward the head of this bay. There at last he stopped, and we made camp.

"The bay teemed with fish, and the sand at its edge was thick with clams. We spent the remaining two hours of daylight gathering berries and digging clams for dinner and gathering wood to use as poles for our tents and to fuel our fire.

"As I worked, I noticed the boy standing knee-deep in the shallow bay, half a dozen yards from shore, looking down into the water. He stood with his waist bent at a right angle, his torso extended forward, his face intent on the water below. He stood that way for quite some time, completely still.

"Then light flashed, the sun glinting off his arm, and there he stood upright, holding a large fish in a fist raised high above his head. A whoop of laughter went up from all of us when we saw it.

"He tossed the fish into the bag that he wore across his shoulders, the one in which he had brought his food. It was soon heavy with four more fish. As the day drew toward darkness, Captain Ferris built a fire while Joe and Nick pitched three tents. The boy had finished his fishing, laid the bag full of his catch beside our tents, and had gone to sit on a boulder at the water's edge. The sun shone off his face as it set.

"As the daylight began to fail, Captain Ferris hurriedly drew his box of matches from its case, struck one of them, and held it to the bits of twig and straw at the base of a stack of kindling. Smoke twirled up the bright orange-red patch amidst the darkening, curling leaves and pine needles, and in an instant, they burst open in flames.

"At that burst of flame the boy suddenly got to his feet on the boulder where he had been sitting. For a minute I thought that he was going to dive off the boulder into the water beside it. But instead he raised both of his arms, holding them straight out from his body to either side, like an acrobat balancing on a *tightrope.*

"He leaned into the wind, then, and steadied himself, all the while staring at the fire. He breathed deeply. He stood that way a long time, until the sun had completely set and the wind dropped, and then the boy, looking suddenly tired, stepped down to the ground again and began walking toward us and the fire."

*

The boy walked directly toward the fire, deliberately, resolutely. As he got close enough to feel the first hints of warmth, his pace slowed. When he came to within an arm's length of the crackling fire, he stopped.

Or, I should say, his feet stopped. But the motion that had begun when he stepped off the boulder continued in his right arm, which he raised, fully extended, so that his hand defined a great arc reaching toward the flame. His hand flexed wide, palm spread open and raised to the fire. The men circling him stared at his hand, knowing the pain that they would feel if they held their hands as close to the fire as he held his.

They were frozen in place by a horrible fascination, watching the boy who did not pull back his hand. When the boy stepped forward again, he walked into the flames that wrapped themselves around him, licking at his shining body.

Marty grabbed at the tent that he and Nick had fashioned from a piece of sailcloth, ripping it from its poles, ready to throw it over the burning boy and smother the flames. But the boy did not come out of the fire. Nor did he collapse in the heat. He stood in the midst of it, revealed. The boy's glass body shone in the firelight. The reflections of the flames surrounding him fluttered and flared in his glass musculature. He smiled.

Then something that looked like beads of molten glass gathered in his eyes and fell into the fire. The boy of glass stood in the flames, crying. After a few minutes, he shook his whole body, as if to bring himself out of some deep reverie and back to the present. He stepped quickly out of the fire.

The men in turn stepped back. The fear they had felt when he had entered the fire, their fear for him as the flames took him, had been replaced by a simpler and more ancient fear. The fabric of the world had burst. And out of the hole that had been torn in the air, nature had spilled terror and beauty that left them helpless.

His body, at once solid and yet subtly fluid,

curving, shone with the deepening blue of the evening sky and the orange-white light of the fire. His face reflected the steady white of the emerging stars, by which, as sailors, they made their living and by which they steered their lives. His face, the same kind of opaque glass known to the Pharaohs of Egypt, seemed to them unimaginably, inexpressibly, incomparably beautiful.

The boy had stepped out of the fire's circle, but stopped just beyond its edge, going no further. He rolled his head in a wide circle, stretching his neck, eyes closed. He wanted to remember this moment, whatever it might mean. He wanted to remember the great relief he felt when he first felt fire. Like sunlight, its energy had fed him, and in it he had felt welcome, as if he belonged there. He wanted to remember how he had lost all capacity for thought, absorbed in the transforming heat.

Then the boy looked up at the five men encircling him. Two of them grasped the edges of a large sheet of canvas tightly, though their hands had fallen to their sides. They looked to the glass boy as if they expected something from him.

He remained standing in that spot by the fire, his own hands at his sides, looking down at his feet, for a long time. Once in a while he would glance up at the horizon, or the moon, or the men, as they slowly got on with their business. When he looked in their direction, he endeavored to look past them, making a show of looking about randomly, as if he were merely looking idly at whatever presented itself to his eyes.

He did not want to face the question on the faces of the men because it was the same question that he wanted to ask of them. He longed for someone to reach for him, not to grasp him but to hold him, to welcome him home. So he decided to ignore them as best he could.

The glass boy turned his thoughts away from the men around him, and he remembered how he had felt in the arms of the fire.

Three

Gus

"As for people like us, you know, it's different if you say you can't always see what we're made of. Then what you mean is that you can't always see in someone's face whether he's lying or not. You can't tell from someone's eyes whether he is looking at you or looking at an idea of you -- maybe his idea of you, or maybe your idea of you that you've been busy laying on him.

"A lot of people -- most people really -- I know they look at me and see some kind of loser. They see an old man crewing on somebody else's boat, and they think, 'Poor old guy, must have got in trouble, lost his way.' They wonder what happened.

"They sort of pity me, I guess, and I know they sure as hell don't want to be me. But I will tell you this: I wouldn't change places with any of these younger guys, not for one minute. They're all full of where they're going. They can't wait till they'll be something. Well, I've been where they are, and I've been where they are going, too: I've even been something more than most of them will ever be. But I wouldn't go back to any of it, not for anything.

"They think I'm lonely, too. I don't even know for sure what 'lonely' means any more. I remember that I used to feel something that I called 'lonely', but for the

life of me I can't really tell what that was any more. I doubt any of them knows what they mean when they say that I must be 'lonely'.

"But that's how it is, you know: people have to have a story about you, especially if you aren't like them to begin with, right? I mean: you're not married and you ain't gonna be: so you're lonely. You're fifty-eight years old and working as a navigator and a cook for some rich guy who's twenty years younger than you: you're a failure or a coward or a fool or a drunk. You're a glass boy and -- well now that's just the point, isn't it? Nobody's got a story to explain that one, to knit him into their scheme of things, to make him another confirmation of them.

"So the boy stood at a little distance from us, not moving at all, until we began to gather around the fire and serve up the dinner. Then as we started to eat, he walked away into the shadows, without even looking over his shoulder at us. For a little while there I thought we just might never see him again.

"And I admit that the idea, even though we were stranded and totally lost without him to guide us, the idea of him disappearing felt a little like relief."

*

The boy turned his back to the fire and walked toward the bay, its quiet water darker even than the night around him. He could feel the energy that the flames had given him still coursing through his limbs, as when the full heart of a mid-summer sun shone on him on his mother's beach. His heavy glass thighs moved easily, his gait deliberate and slow.

The cold, soft mud along the shoreline pulled at his feet as he waded out into the shallow water, and the wetter mud, slimy between his toes, dragged him down till he had sunk up to his calves. He widened his stance, then, stabilized himself in the moving water, and stood in the dark. He breathed deeply, smelling the sea. It smelled like home.

The boy stood in the water throughout the night. Slowly the energy he had absorbed from the fire seeped away from his glass flesh and into the cool night air. As he grew more and more tired, he found himself remembering the water at his mother's door when he had first stepped out into the wild winds and beheld the storm. For a time he felt almost undone by a longing to return to his mother, to his home and the sea. But whenever that longing lifted itself up into the form of thought, he remembered what she had said about his father, that he lived among men, and he felt a longing even more powerful, a hunger to know his father. He had made his way this far by directing his steps away from the smell of the sea and toward the smell of the land, which was for him merely the absence of the sea in the dry, offshore wind.

At dawn, the light of the rising sun struck him where he stood sleeping. The light penetrated him, and in a process akin both to photosynthesis and to the effect of light on the silicon wafer at the heart of a photo-voltaic cell, his flesh began to transform the light's energy into the energy of life. The glass boy soon stirred from his slumber and started to walk slowly back to the shore, the mud sucking at his feet, trying to hold him, not wanting to let him go.

As he rose out of the water, he looked down at his legs and saw the mud coating his calves and ankles and feet. He liked that he could smell the salt water in the mud, a hint of the sea that stayed with him. He thought of the beautiful flecks of light in his mother's face. He lowered his head and walked back toward the camp.

*

Nick
"All you gotta do is look at a guy like that and you know he's going to be important. He's the kind of guy you could make a fortune just hanging around. People are gonna want to know somebody like that. And if they know that you're a friend of his, they're gonna

want to know you, too. And if they want to get near him bad enough, you're gonna be able to ask them for anything.

"It's not like I'm cheating him in any way. It's the others who are paying. And on top of that, he saved my life, which some people say means he's responsible for me from here on out. No way its my fault I'm here now, and what I do and what happens to me is because he saved me. He's gotta take care of me since he's responsible for me still being alive.

"I pretty much figured it out from the first moment I saw him.

"From that first moment on the beach, I kept my eye on him. When opportunity knocks, you gotta open the door, right? I wasn't gonna let this one out of my sight, not ever. I made sure I didn't miss a thing. I saw when he clambered up that cliff, and I followed him right away. I didn't know he was glass, not yet, but I knew he wasn't exactly like any human being I ever saw. I knew he was something nobody else had ever seen either, and I knew that probably for the rest of my life he would be the most important thing that ever happened to me.

"I always focused on him first and let other things catch my eye only when they started to have something to do with him. It's all about keeping your focus, about not missing the main chance when it comes around to you. Lots of guys have great opportunities come their way, but if you don't stay focused and grab it when it comes, you end up being a loser.

"I stayed right by him. The whole rest of the day and the one after that, I was glued to his side. We hiked from our camp at the head of that narrow bay up along the hills to the south. It was a hell of a lot hotter because we were moving inland. As the sun got higher, we were glad the hills were wooded so at least we had some shade. Funny, but the kid didn't seem to be bothered by the heat at all. If anything, that blazing sun seemed to invigorate him.

"We reached the ridge pretty quick. That was when I realized that the ridge we'd been climbing was the back side of Twin Peaks. We came up its western slope. The trees thinned as we came up to the ridge. It was the really hot part of the day, the late afternoon, and we were all getting pretty tired. We were all trying to keep up, but we all occasionally stopped to catch a breath and turn around and look back to the west and see the ocean. The glare almost blinded you.

"The wind really whipped up that western slope. The trees got more like the ones we'd seen when we first got up to the top of the cliffs, all gnarled and twisted, like some kind of weird creature's arms and legs. Near the top of the slope the trees stopped completely, and the wind seemed to be carrying us up the mountainside. It was making me feel light, like we were sailing."

*

The glass boy was the first of the small band to crest the ridge at the notch between the Twin Peaks. He stopped short at the sight opening below him, and the others gathered around him as they arrived. The eastern slope dropped away quickly from the promontory on which they stood. Just below them, a herd of cows grazed on open grassland. Below that, the slope was covered by houses which descended further into a valley full of traffic and noise, at the edge of a huge city that sprawled for miles to the waters of a vast bay beyond.

As he had walked inland, the boy who was made of glass had come to understand that the hills were the waves of the earth. Though seemingly inert, the ground, as he saw in the shapes of the terrain, was flowing too, however slowly. This understanding had brought him comfort as he traveled further and further from his mother and his home.

The dry land that she had taught him to fear, however strange, did not oppose the sea that he loved and knew so well. The land was but a continuation of the sea in another form. And now he stood on the crest of a massive wave of land, the Twin Peaks, and looked down on something altogether different from both the sea and the land: The City.

Not only had he never seen anything like it, but he knew that he could not even have imagined it. Thrusting up from the earth, not rolling like a wave but stabbing up into the sky, the prodigious mass of glass and steel defied everything around it: the water, the flatlands and wetlands, the hills, the mountains, even the sky.

The sight thrilled the glass boy with the conflicted beauty that it displayed. It thrilled him with its evocation of power, demanding as it did a position among the elemental forces. What is more, in its straight lines, angles, and facets, its rigidity and its way with the light, he recognized something akin to his own nature. The sun lowering behind the boy shot orange-rose flashes that fired off the thousand thousand windows in the houses and the towers below.

The City seemed to pull at all the myriad activity in the landscape around it, dragging everything in toward itself and holding as much of it as it could at its heart, a huge mass of glass towers. On the other side of the dense thicket of towers, the shining, blue bay opened inland, its sparkling waters spanned by five massive bridges. On the far shore, mountains rose higher and higher to the east, in ranges that stretched from north to south as far as the eye could see.

The boy stood transfixed by the sight of The City. The towers appeared to him to be sleeping giants who were made of the same stuff that he was made of, standing shoulder to shoulder beside the water below. Their faceted surfaces glittered in the ruddy light of the declining sun.

Perhaps his father had returned to this place, and perhaps now he stood among those giants, somewhere in the busy city below. Someone might be able to tell him about his father, perhaps someone could even tell the boy where to find him. If not, then at least one of the giants might know something about him. They might even be his relatives, an unknown family to which he, the boy who was made of glass, was about to be restored.

The glass boy started to laugh. Then he thought of the look his mother had given him when they both understood that he would not give up his quest for her sake. He stopped laughing. He had hurt his mother, he knew, and he had broken the unquestioned bond of trust that had held them together throughout all of his young life, until now.

Much had been lost in the last three days, both for the shipwrecked men and for the glass boy, and perhaps more, much more, would be lost in The City below. As the glass boy's laughter trailed off into silence, the men heard only the thin tinkling sound they had heard from him occasionally over the last three days, a sound that as yet meant nothing in their ears.

PART TWO

When I was a child, I spake as a child, I thought as a child: but when I became a man, I put away childish things. For now we see as through a glass, darkly . . .

[I Corinthians 13:11-12]

Four

There was a time when men like William Ferris III, content with being called "Captains of Industry", had felt no particular need to command any vessel that was actually seaworthy. They left the sailboats, as well as the polo ponies, to certain aristocratic relics of the useless past, whom they called "playboys." They prided themselves instead on being businessmen and held themselves superior to men who owed their wealth to a mere accident of birth.

If William Ferris III's grandfather, plain Will Ferris, had made his first million dollars as early in life as William III had made his first ten million, he might, at most, have chartered a yacht and hired a crew to sail him down to Catalina Island, so that he could play Blackjack all night at the Avalon Casino. But times change, and William Ferris III always preferred to take the helm himself. He liked to think of himself as one of a new breed: a man who played as hard as he worked, a man who sought out new challenges, new opportunities to overcome difficulty and even danger. He might have inherited a fortune, but he would see to it that no one could call him lazy.

"Billy", as both his friends and the global media called him, especially relished any challenge that demanded both physical strength and mental acuity, particularly if that challenge involved competition with other rich and powerful men amid high-profile news coverage. The annual sailing race up the coast fitted his needs perfectly, and although he had now technically lost the race, in as much as his boat lay in pieces along stretches of the north coast, he felt sure that in the end he had won something much bigger than a mere trophy.

As the small band was hiking from the distant shore to The City, Billy had ruminated on his situation. The media coverage of his disappearance in the freak storm on the last night of the race would be full-blown, and his impending heroic return would pay off in further publicity worth millions of dollars to his company, SpinWare, and to himself. This opportunity brought with it certain risks, however, which Billy had been weighing almost since he had first glimpsed the firelight dancing on the glass boy's shining face in the shadows on the beach.

Unfortunately, Billy was not certain that his apparent failure (had lost the race and his boat, after all) would be forgotten amid his joyful return, even bringing all four of his men home alive and well. But if he played it right, his loss might very well be obliterated by the sixth who came with them: he had discovered a creature of immense scientific interest and had brought this creature back to The City, something that amounted to an historic discovery.

This outcome would, however, require a *finesse*: how much Billy's survival and return he owed to the boy himself must not become the subject of public inquiry. Billy might inwardly pride himself on keeping a debt of honor to the boy, by giving him everything that he might want, but his beneficence should appear to be a matter of his own integrity, and not an obligation adhered to out of regard for public opinion. Billy felt certain that he would prove to be a very good man.

Now, standing atop Twin Peaks, Billy took in the commanding view of The City as he tried to estimate the current state of information about, and interest in, his disappearance. He imagined that the public's anxiety might be great. Billy was also aware that, as flattering as such full-blown attention might be to him personally, the possibility that William Ferris III might never return would sink SpinWare's share price as surely as the freak storm had sunk his boat. Furthermore, the uncertainty would disturb SpinWare employees and diminish their productivity.

And while his triumphant return would repair much of the damage, he could not afford to leave any lingering doubts about his leadership abilities. He had lost control of his boat, and it had sunk from under him. No one must think that SpinWare might share the fate.

Billy had trained himself to view risks as opportunities, despite the fact that such jingoistic optimism was antithetical to his true nature. So for the past two days he spent the hours of hiking under the hot sun, and the hours of lying awake under the astonishingly starry night, shoring up his courage with an image of himself: the discoverer of new life; the savior of a lost boy.

Now, as he came to stand beside the glass boy looking out over The City and the bay beyond, he felt confident of success. Billy was ready to take control of the situation. He stepped around in front of the boy and began to speak.

"I don't know how you knew that this is our home and that this is where we needed to be led, but I thank you from the bottom of my heart for bringing us here. My guess is that you have never been here before. Is that right? I'm pretty sure that everyone would have heard of you if you had ever visited The City before."

Nick, who was standing beside the boy of glass and following his skipper's words intently, smiled.

"Am I right? Or have you, in fact, been here before?" Billy asked.

The boy looked down at his feet. He began to tell them about his mother's warnings against wandering far from home and about his sense that her fears were overblown, but the men heard only a light, airy tinkling, as of shards of glass knocked softly against one another.

Billy continued to speak regardless of whether the boy could understand him. Although he addressed the boy, his words were meant for the ears of the whole company.

"I will be happy -- will be honored -- to be your guide to our world, our City, our home," Billy said. "Let me show you everything," he continued, gesturing out over The City, the bay, and the mountains beyond.

The boy looked up again and said, "Thank you." The wind had dropped momentarily,

51

and the din from the busy traffic below seemed to fall away in the lull. For the first time Billy thought that he could make out the words formed by the delicate voice emanating from the boy. "I want so much to find my father," the boy said.

But Billy understood only the first four words of the glass boy's sentence, and charging ahead before the boy had finished speaking, Billy said with a laugh, "Of course you do!"

"Who doesn't want much?" Billy continued. "Who doesn't want it all? Don't worry, my friend, you shall have very much, practically everything you could want."

Marty had been watching Ferris's performance with a thin smile that came dangerously close to a smirk. But Nick continued to look on with real pleasure. Nick felt happy for the boy, imagining the immense resources that the rich man would lay at the feet of their new friend. He continued to listen attentively as Billy set forth his plans, listening for an opening for himself.

"First, we all know how dangerous it would be if you" -- Billy was addressing the glass boy -- "were subjected to the crush of news-hounds and celebrity chasers. You must not simply appear in The City without some preparation -- on both sides," Billy said.

Marty, Gus, and Joe listened with stony faces, unmoved except for a slight deepening of the pinched crease on Marty's forehead.

"I am," Billy went on, "obviously the one most qualified to handle the press and the public, so that no problems or misconceptions arise. But while I handle those preparations," and here Billy looked to the other men, his crew, as if his question were not merely rhetorical. "What shall we do to see that he is taken care of?"

Joe stood to one side, listing slightly to the right, having shifted his weight entirely onto that leg while the left leg traced an arc in the dusty earth on the barren peak. Marty and Gus held their silence. Nick grinned but said nothing.

"Nick, don't you live in this neighborhood?" Billy asked.

"I sure do! If you go right down Twenty-Fifth Street there," Nick answered, pointing down the hillside, "well, it's kind of hard to see just how the street goes but toward the hospital --"

Billy cut him off. "As long as you know how

to get there, Nick, I'm sure I don't need to find it. Do you think you could take our friend to your home until I have made preparations for his introduction to The City?"

"Hell, yes!" Nick said, recovering the bright expression that had momentarily dimmed while Billy spoke. Marty gave a disgusted snort, which he quickly covered by pulling a handkerchief from his pocket and pretending to sniffle and blow his nose.

"Great," Billy said to Nick. "Thanks for your help."

Nick grinned, standing beside the glass boy. Marty and Gus stood by silently. Joe continued using his toe to draw and redraw that lazy arc in the dust in front of him, seeming not to have heard a word. The glass boy stood gazing down on The City glittering in the afternoon sun.

*

As the band of six picked their way down the steep eastern flank of Twin Peaks, the glass boy watched his feet kick loose bits of rock and gravel that then raced ahead of him, bouncing and tumbling down the rocky hillside. When they reached the grassy pasture land, he looked up and into the eyes of the one of the cows in the small herd who looked back at him and followed him with her big liquid eyes. Soon Nick and the glass boy separated from the rest and turned south, toward the edge of the woods, while the others continued to move directly eastward, toward the *cul de sac* at the top of Clipper Street. Nick walked quickly, and the glass boy, no longer leading but following in Nick's footsteps, lengthened his stride to keep up.

Nick had wanted to talk to the boy since first catching sight of him in the shadows of that night on the beach. But once the other men had seen the boy too, Nick had kept silent. At nineteen, Nick had found by experience that the best strategy in any new situation, when there was always a risk of breaking rules that he had not even known existed, was to watch what other men did before making any move himself. "Never be the first to do anything," he told himself. He did not want to get ahead of anybody. He had learned that men can give you all the rope you need and then leave you hanging out there on your own.

Now that he was alone with the boy of glass, Nick no longer needed to hold his tongue.

"You're really gonna like this place I got," he

said, turning his head to call back over his shoulder to the glass boy. "The apartment itself is kind of dark because it's a basement and everything, but you walk in and -- you'll see -- it's like the first thing you see is this wall of glass. The whole back side of the apartment looks out into the garden, and I've fixed it up like a living room outside. It's awesome, man. Really cool. And my landlord, he's like just really, really cool, you know?"

Nick was not entirely sure that the boy could understand his words, but he rambled on because he was one of those people who feels uncomfortable with silence in the company of others. In fact, Nick was not entirely comfortable with silence when he was alone, either. He often talked to himself even while hiking alone through these very woods. His monologues usually kept him cheerful in his solitude, but this time, hearing the breeze into which his words faded away, Nick shivered.

As they reached the edge of the woods, Nick stopped still and turned to the boy of glass behind him. Had he said something? Or had that sound been only the wind? Nick looked intently into the boy's shining face. The cumulative exhaustion of the hours fighting the storm at sea, first on the boat and then in the water, compounded by the ensuing three day's journey, suddenly caught up with him. Nick wavered a bit, as if he might fall asleep right where he stood. He shook his head to ward off the spell.

"Of course," he said, returning his thoughts to the home toward which they were making their way, "We'll still have to get you in without him seeing you -- the landlord, I mean."

The boy looked at Nick, tilting his head slightly to one side.

"Well, at least just at first, you know. Like the skipper said, you gotta break 'em in easy."

Nick looked into the glass face as he spoke, seeing the immense blue of the sky behind him and the messy-haired silhouette of his own head, which fell as a shadow across the boy's cheekbones, nose, mouth, jaw, neck. Nick titled his own head a bit to the left, to check whether the dark form he saw reflected on or in the boy of glass was indeed his own.

He moved. It moved. It was his.

The shadow of his own head prevented Nick from seeing the glass boy's mouth. But he heard something rattle in the breeze, as if the sound of the ocean's chill were carried on the air from far away, wrapping itself around the back of his neck and climbing the back of his skull, and his shoulders jerked with a quick, sharp shudder.

"You don't know what people are like, do you?" Nick said, still staring into the glass face. It occurred to him that, unattended, the kid might innocently approach people and cause panic. Someone might shoot the glass boy out of blind fear. Anything could happen, and he was the only one who would be keeping an eye out.

Nick feared carrying a responsibility that he had not really thought through. For a moment he felt as though he might throw up. He could not catch his breath, the wind having been knocked out of him as surely as it had been when he first hit the icy water when the boat broke apart beneath him. He had to grab air with his mouth and force it down into his lungs.

The moment passed. Nick began to breathe more easily again. He would be home soon. They had only a short distance -- two miles at most.

But there was something wrong with the relief that he felt. It reminded him of something, but what? Nick tried to think through the last few days and realized for the first time that he had no memory of the actual breaking up of the boat or of the final hour they had spent under sail. All he remembered of the disaster was that as he regained consciousness on the beach, he had tasted sand in his mouth and felt its grains in his teeth.

Nick shook his head slowly, gazing at the glass boy.

"Man," he said, "am I gonna have to look out for you."

The boy stood with his head turned away from Nick, looking down at The City. Nick waited for the boy to turn to follow him again and, when he did not, put his hand on the boy's shoulder. The boy turned from his reverie, and Nick began leading him toward the dark thicket ahead of them and into the woods beyond.

*

They had to duck through a low opening in the bushes to enter the thicket. Once inside, they found themselves on a narrow footpath worn into the carpet of grasses, plantain, lupine, and oxalis. The latter were in bloom, their little yellow heads bouncing and nodding as they passed.

59

"Nobody comes in here," Nick said in the hushed voice he would have used in a library or a church. "Well, nobody but stoners. There's a school at the bottom of the hill and the kids who cut class come up here to get high and shit."

Nick felt self-conscious when he heard the vulgar word coming from his lips, and he glanced over his shoulder at the boy, whose dark face was completely blank in the shadows of the woods. It occurred to Nick that the boy might not have understood what he was saying. The kid had said something to Billy up on the ridge, but Nick wasn't sure just how good the stranger's English might be. At least the glass boy didn't seem offended by what Nick had just said.

Nick turned to look ahead again and resumed leading the boy through the woods. Behind him, the glass boy looked up into the trees whispering overhead. Then he lifted each foot and looked at the soles of his feet. When he continued following Nick, he watched his step along the path ahead of him carefully.

"It's gonna get kinda steep ahead," Nick said, "but then I guess I don't need to worry about you and cliffs, hunh?"

The boy said nothing. Nick shrugged his shoulders and walked on, slowly. They were approaching a sheer rock face that dropped about seventy-five feet to the street below, with tangled vines of wild berries clinging to the hillside as it dropped away.

"I'm glad we've still got some light to do this by," Nick said as he prepared to pick his way down the series of narrow ledges that constituted the path down the cliff. "But it will be much easier to get you all the way down the valley to my place after it is dark, that's for sure."

The wind was picking up as the sun lowered in the west. As it did, it was diverted around Twin Peaks, picking up velocity and blowing hard down the hillside and through the woods. It whipped the incoming fog through the trees, tearing it into hanks of moist, pale cloud that swirled around them. "Jeeze!" Nick said with a shudder. "It's getting hella cold. And it's not gonna get really dark for another hour."

They picked their way down the cliff, which had been formed by men who had quarried from this hillside the stone with which to build The City a century before. That old City, the one built of stone, had, for the most part, been replaced by the steel and glass towers of the new skyline. A few remnants of that earlier town huddled in the odd corners and lost alleys, where they managed to survive, overshadowed even at noon. And here the land that had been so deeply cut and had felt great chunks of itself being ripped away, now grew ferns and wild berries, poison oak, broad-leaved grasses, and towering cypresses and oaks that shaded all. Fog gathered in the foliage and dripped onto the softening rock.

They were standing at the bottom of the cliff, just inside the edge of the park, where the woods give way to the macadam of Douglass Street and rectilinear landscape of The City. Nick's clenched fist held the collar of his shirt closed tightly around his neck, and he hunched his shoulders to keep warm. He took a long look at the glass boy, who stood beside him calm and upright, as if untouched by the cold.

"Damn it," Nick said. He stood silently shivering for a minute or two and then added, "Let's get outta here."

Nick at that moment felt the twinge of foreboding that comes when we know we are breaking our word. He had told the skipper that he would not let anyone else see the boy, but the cold wind was much stronger than his twinge of regret. He had not even thought of Johnnie until he had mentioned the kids from the school getting stoned in the woods. After all, if he had thought of Johnnie's place when they were all still at the top of the hill, Nick would have mentioned it to the skipper, who would have agreed that it wouldn't cause any problems. The skipper would have OK'd them keeping out of sight at Johnnie's, for sure.

So Nick straightened himself up and spoke to the glass boy with confidence. "Johnnie's cool. You'll see. He's always home; so there's no problem dropping in." Nick hesitated before he continued. "There's one thing I gotta tell you right off, though: he's a dealer. But don't worry. It's cool. You'll see. In fact, that's why it's so perfect. Johnnie wouldn't say anything about you to anybody because the last thing he wants to do is draw attention to himself at all in any way."

Nick took a couple of steps beyond the edge of the trees and into the street so that he could see whether anyone was coming. Only the tattered fog scuttled through the air across the expanse of pavement now wet and black. He signaled to the boy with a circular motion of his arm to come out of the woods and follow him across the street. Together they entered the shallow doorway and stood at

Johnnie's gate.

Nick pressed the buzzer.

＊

Johnnie's voice came through a small speaker beside the gate. "Who are you?"

"Hey Johnnie, it's just Nick. I was wondering if I could stop by."

"Nickie!" Johnnie shouted, almost blowing out the scratchy little speaker entirely. "Jesus, Nick, get the hell in here!"

The lock buzzed, and Nick pushed the gate open. As they crossed the small inner courtyard, he and the boy could hear Johnnie shouting through the as yet unopened door. "Stop by? Stop by? You're fucking alive, man!"

The door opened. In the instant it took Johnnie to see that Nick was not alone, his exuberant greeting was cut short. His wiry frame stiffened, and his eyes narrowed.

Johnnie had obvious reasons to guard his privacy closely. He always insisted that Nick or anyone else who wanted to bring a friend along check with him in advance. In the half-dozen years that Nick had known Johnnie, he had been in the house only twice when someone had made the mistake of bringing an uninvited guest. On those occasions Johnnie exploded in a rage few could imagine, and both the erstwhile friend and the stranger were sent away, forbidden ever to return.

As the door opened, Johnnie's smiling lips clenched, and Nick braced himself for the worst. Johnnie opened his mouth, but instead of venting a storm of curses and rage, the mouth just hung slack. Above it, Johnnie's eyes relaxed and opened wide. Nick did not see it, but Johnnie felt them moisten as he saw the glass boy for the first time.

"I hope it's OK, Johnnie," Nick said timidly. "This guy rescued us that night in the storm. It's cool. You'll see."

Johnnie said nothing. His mouth closed, and he took a step back into his house, holding the door open and allowing the two to enter. He began to smile as they passed. He closed the door behind them, and still without a word, he followed them into his living room, where he motioned for them to sit on the couch while he pulled his big armchair closer and sat opposite them.

Johnnie usually leaned back in that chair, as if

65

it were a throne, conducting conversations, and business, with an air of genial authority. Johnnie made people happy, or at least his product did. People wanted to be near him, and he orchestrated them, making a party out of random visitors, for however long they stayed.

Johnnie had been holding court in just such a fashion when Nick first buzzed at the gate. Ever cautious, Johnnie had sent the two young men with whom he had been smoking and talking into the back parlor to watch videos before he rose to go to the door. Truth be told, these videos had been the men's primary objective when they came to visit Johnnie.

For twenty years the guys in the neighborhood had been telling their wives, girlfriends, or "significant others" that they were going over to Johnnie's to watch TV with their friends. They had not really lied: they were indeed watching the television. But what they were watching on the TV was Johnnie's ever-growing collection of pornography, first on Betamax, then on VHS, and now on DVD. Johnnie had arranged the furniture, the plants, and a Chinese lacquered screen so that he could keep an eye on things from his armchair as they watched.

Nick had grown up in the neighborhood and had watched his share of Johnnie's videos. He had tried some of Johnnie's merchandise, too. But Nick never took to it the way some of the other guys did. Some of them took to it so strongly that the look in their eyes scared Nick. Despite the fact that Johnnie was neither famous nor rich, he was, indeed, influential: Johnnie had changed some lives.

"OK," Johnnie said, addressing Nick without ever taking his eyes off the glass boy. "You gotta tell me the story, Nick, the whole story."

Nick drew a deep breath. "Well. We were on our third day out, you know --"

"Yeah, yeah," Johnnie cut in. "Sudden storm and you disappear from GPS, lost at sea, shipwreck: that's all that's been on the news for the last three days, Nick. I know all that shit already. I wanna know the real story, Nickie boy," Johnnie said, taking his eyes from the glass boy and looking at Nick for the first time since he had opened the door.

"Well, we made it," Nick said, the life gone out of his voice. Not only had Johnnie cut him off, but he was troubled by the realization, again, that he could not actually remember what had happened during the storm. "And we met him there on the beach

67

where we wrecked --" Nick was beginning to feel the chill of real fear when he tried to think back to what had happened in the storm and his mind met only emptiness.

"He helped you out?" Johnnie asked, trying to get Nick's attention.

"Yeah, like he showed us how to get up the cliffs from the beach and how to make our way back here to The City."

"He knew the way here?" Johnnie asked, watching the boy of glass again, intently. "He's been here before?"

"Shit no," Nickie said with a laugh. "Why the hell would the Skipper be so worried about keeping him hidden if anybody had seen him before?"

Johnnie began, slowly, to smile, and his words came softly, hushed almost to a whisper. "So Ferris is keeping the kid on ice?" he asked.

Nick fidgeted in his chair. The sense of comfort he had felt when he first gained access to the warm house and to Johnnie's hospitality was waning. "Well, sure, Johnnie. You know, the media and the mayor and security issues -- Jeeze, can you imagine what the Homeland guys --"

68

At the word "Homeland", Johnnie shot a glance at Nick, and Nick felt his happiness sink into his belly. He half expected the fury that might have met them at the door to explode from Johnnie at the mention of the government agency. But the wince that distorted Johnnie's face brought with it an idea, and Johnnie relaxed and eased back into the comfort of his deep chair.

"You brought your friend to the right place, Nickie my boy. Yes indeed. I can and will do all I can to help you out -- both of you. No one sees what happens here, Nickie, not even Homeland Security."

The silence that followed relieved Nick without relaxing him and allowed Johnnie to sink deeper into his chair and into his thoughts.

Johnnie had been watching the glass boy for all but a few seconds of the time since they had arrived at his house. But while he had been watching, he had failed to look. Having failed to look, he had failed to see. In the silence, Johnnie now began to see.

Looking into the dark glass face, Johnnie slowly came to feel as though he were floating on the ceiling of his own living room, looking

69

down at himself and at Nick and the boy of glass. He shook his head to regain his equilibrium, but Johnnie's sense of reality slipped from him again almost immediately. He told himself that the sensation of floating resulted from the distortions in the reflection of the room, and of Johnnie himself, in the glass boy's face.

Johnnie found himself remembering an Art History course he had taken, and loved, in his only year at the University. He remembered a painting of a bride and groom who stood in a room that was repeated and distorted in a convex mirror hanging on the wall behind them, a painting by Jan Van Something. He tried to remember the name but instead remembered an afternoon walk back to his dorm room when the quality of the light that shot through the deep sky from the setting sun cut the edges of every building, the stone edges of the bell tower, and even the edges of every leaf on every eucalypt and every needle on every pine. He remembered feeling a thrill in his chest at the clarity of the sight.

Then Johnnie remembered the smell of the hallway in the dorm and the dimness of his little room, only half of which was his. A narrow bed, a table, a single lamp. That spring his father had died, and Johnnie did not return the following fall. His education had ended.

"Old John must really be high this time," he thought to himself. He knew that he had not really smoked all that much, since the guys had arrived only a few minutes before Nick had buzzed at the door. Still, maybe he should just cut it out completely for a few days, he thought, as if that were easy, as if he had ever been able to quit before.

Something big was going on, big enough to have Billy Ferris himself working overtime. And Nick had brought it right through Johnnie's own front door. It would pay to stay on his toes for this one. He might be able to work something sweet, something really sweet. Johnnie leaned forward again, smiling at the glass boy, but he could read no expression at all on the dark, gleaming face.

*

William Ferris III, billionaire deal-maker, entrepreneur, horseman, art collector, gentleman rancher, and yachtsman, had been lost at sea for seventy-two hours when he walked into the clock repair shop at the corner of Sanchez and Twenty-Sixth Streets. It was the first place of business Billy had found that was open that afternoon. The owner of the shop, an old Irishman, looked up from his work at the bench in the back and peered at Billy over his half-rim glasses.

"Can I help you?" he called out, as he unfolded his arthritic knees and rose, with help of a mahogany cane, to his feet. Before Billy could answer, the old man had shuffled sufficiently toward the light at the front of the store to see who stood before him, and he burst into a joyous laugh.

"Dear God!" he cried out. "You're alive, man!" He laughed again as he hurried his shuffling feet along, steadying himself with his cane and thrusting his right hand forward for Billy to shake. Billy politely extended his own hand, and the wizened Irishman pumped it heartily.

"Well Good Lord," he continued. "Lord, Lord, look at you. You look fine, my man, mighty well. With what you have been through, well, amazing. Yes, Sir, mighty lucky, Sir, mighty lucky."

He leaned back and took a long look at his famous guest. Billy jumped when the old man suddenly shouted "What am I doing lollygagging like this! I've got to call 911! They need to know that you've come through, man. My God they have been worrying themselves sick. Everyone has been worrying and praying all along, hoping and praying that God would see you home, even though --"

Billy cut him off abruptly by holding up his open palm like a policeman stopping traffic. Then he dropped his hand and spoke reassuringly. "I mean, thank you. Thank you. Truly. Thank you. But what I need right now is to use the phone myself. That is," Billy said, "if you would be so kind as to allow me to use your telephone."

The shop-owner had seemed to slump within himself, as if seeing the television lights bypass his shop. He would now have no role in the return of the great man. But he perked up when Billy had so politely asked his favor, and he now scurried toward the back of the store saying "Why, yes, Sir! Of course, Sir! Why it's right here, Sir, right here on the table back here."

With the cane that he held in his left hand, the little man swept from the table an old cat, a twenty-five pound calico cat, while with his right hand he reached under a heap of old receipts, trade magazines, and yellowed newspapers to fish out the phone. He found it, and with both hands held it up like an offering for the great man to take: a heavy, black Bakelite telephone, its metal dial suspended over a gleaming white circle of numbers.

Billy clapped his hands together in front of his face, holding them together palm to palm. He looked into the eyes of his host as if acknowledging some bond between them. He had not seen one of these in many, many years.

Billy remembered disassembling phones like this in his childhood, taking them apart and putting them back together, finding discarded phones that didn't work and repairing them in his room late into the night. He remembered phones, and then he remembered phone switches; phone switches and then computers; modems and then routers; and finally software: he had come all the way from a boy's excitement over an old phone like this one to being who he was: celebrity CEO Billy Ferris.

As he took the telephone from the old man's upraised hands, Billy was surprised to feel how heavy the metal and Bakelite object was. The ancient telephone was cold, too, almost icy to the touch, and Billy felt a shiver run up his arms as the phone sank into his palms. The past was coming up behind Billy, coming up behind him like a wave, a great wave that had already broken on the shore and was running up the sand, a thinning film of bitter cold sea-water lapping at Billy's heels.

"There you are, Sir," the old man said.

Five

Marty, Joe, and Gus stood on the sidewalk in front of the clock repair shop while Billy made his call. "Louis!" they heard Billy exclaim when his personal assistant answered. "Louis, my man, I've got something big this time."

Gus looked at Marty, who rolled his eyes. Joe stood with his eyes closed, his lips moving silently in what the other two knew was prayer.

"That's very kind, Louis, but I don't mean my survival. I mean something much bigger. I know. I know. OK, but now listen. None of that matters. They always love me. Remember? Even when they hate me, they love me. Right, Louis? I give them something to write about.

"OK. So this time they are really and truly going to love me. They not only get danger and survival and everyone home safe this time, Louis. They get 'heroic' this time. But Louis -- slow down Louis -- I'm talking about something even bigger than that. I'm talking 'historic' -- not as in 'stock at new high', either, but as in 'tell your grandchildren where you were when you first heard'.

Billy's voice dropped almost to a whisper, and for a minute the three men outside could not make out his words. Then Billy's voice rose again as he finished the call.

"OK. Now I need to get to the office to make some calls, and I need to get cleaned up before anyone knows that I'm back. That's it.

"What? Yes, that's right. 10:00 am tomorrow. But until then no one is to know that I am back, not even Sarah," Billy said, referring to his then-current wife. "No one, Louis. Clear?"

Billy hung up the phone, replacing the heavy handset in its elegantly curved cradle and handing the machine with reverence back to the Irishman. Then he stepped out onto the sidewalk to tell his crew that Louis would be arriving soon with a car to take them all to the office downtown.

Gus and Marty blurted out "You're kidding" in unison wile Joe cried out "My Siria!" so loudly that Billy looked angrily around to see whether anyone was looking. Tears flowed down Joe's face.

Billy immediately softened his stance and reached out to put a hand on Joe's shoulder.

Joe jerked away from Billy's touch and stood staring at his feet.

"Look, Joe," Billy said in a soothing tone. "And you guys too, Gus, Marty. We're all eager to get home. And we're all exhausted. My God, don't you think I want to see Sarah more than anything in the world?"

Joe calmed down a little at these words, while Gus and Marty kept to themselves their thoughts about the relative likelihood that Billy Ferris might be eager to see his wife.

*

Johnnie leaned all the way back in his chair and brought his hands together almost to a position of prayer, keeping the palms apart as fingertips touched. He looked over the tented fingers at Nick.

"So Nicky, I'm sorry I cut you off in the middle of your story. I do want to know the whole story, OK? Don't I always want to know the whole story? I think I just got anxious because right now I want to do whatever I can to help you guys out. That's my number one priority right now: helping out." Johnnie turned his face toward the glass boy, although he avoided looking directly at him.

77

"Captain Ferris asked me to keep him at my place, you know," Nick said, "so people don't see him and get all weirded out or shit, you know? I mean, can you imagine? He -- the skipper I mean -- he wants to hold a press conference to introduce him and make it easier for him by kinda getting people ready." Nick's voice rose on the last two words as if his sentence had been a question.

If Nick had thought about the implications of the Ferris plan, he would have had to admit that the boy of glass hardly needed protection at all. As far as Nick had seen, the boy could take care not only of himself but of everyone who came in contact with him. Even Johnnie had been calmed by his presence.

Johnnie himself, however, understood what Mr. Ferris might think he needed to do with the glass boy.

"Sounds to me like the guy knows what he's doing, Nicky. He's certainly got a lot more experience with the press that you or I do, right?" Johnnie was looking toward the boy as he spoke, but he did not raise his eyes to look into the glass face. He was not going to take that chance again, at least not for now.

"Besides," Johnnie said, turning once more to

Nick, "He's the Captain, right? And everybody else? We're all just his crew."

Nick almost corrected Johnnie, but fear of showing any disrespect held him back. Johnnie was the only man Nick had ever known -- not just worked for or saw at school or in church, but actually known -- who commanded real authority among others. People cared what Johnnie thought of them. They wanted his approval. They did things for Johnnie that Johnnie had not even asked them to do.

"Thanks, man." Nick said. "We really needed a place to hang till it gets dark and we can walk over to my place."

"Well this is the perfect place to hang out," said one of the two neighborhood men whom Johnnie had earlier sent to the back room.

Nick had caught sight of the young man's bright red hoodie out of the corner of his eye as the fellow had sauntered into the living room. Johnnie, however, had not. The unexpected voice speaking close behind Johnnie almost catapulted him onto the glass boy. Johnnie literally leapt to his feet, seeming to spin in mid-air, and instantly he was staring into the young man's face, his nose not two inches from the guy's nose.

79

Johnnie was all nerve and sinew even at the best of times, and now he held his thin frame locked so tightly that his muscles vibrated. The young man's bravado vanished and was replaced by something close to panic.

Johnnie spoke in a measured, menacing tone. "I distinctly remember telling you not, not -- get it? -- not to come into this room until and unless I called you in. Do you remember?"

The young man stared at his feet. Johnnie ran his finger around the rim of a crystal bowl that sat on the end table by sofa, trying to master the trembling. As he did, the tension appeared to flow directly into the young man's body as it left Johnnie's.

The neighbor, keeping his head down, muttered that he would go back to the other room. He left without having actually looked at the boy of glass.

Through the gap between the lacquered screen and the edge of the kitchen wall, Nick could see the guy return to his companion in the bedroom who looked up suddenly as he came in. Then they both moved inward and out of sight.

Johnnie remained standing and, now calm,

said "Let's go upstairs. It's always too busy down here."

Nick had only twice before been invited upstairs at Johnnie's, and he felt proud to have earned another invitation. Downstairs at Johnnie's was public, even if the guests were carefully screened. But upstairs was Johnnie's private life. If Johnnie included you upstairs, you could count yourself a friend. Johnnie was clearly taken with the glass boy, and any doubts Nick might have felt earlier about the wisdom of breaking his word to his skipper were washed away by Johnnie's hospitality.

Nick felt happier still to be taking the glass boy upstairs, not for the honor, which he suspected the boy would not understand, but for the view. Johnnie's bedroom bowed out on the north side of the house, and the curved wall, floor to ceiling, was glass. The City, and the whole of the bay that surrounded its northern and eastern flanks, and even the hills on the far shores of that bay and the distant mountains rising beyond, lay at the feet of anyone who stood in Johnnie's upper room.

The three figures stood looking out on The City sparkling in the last of the afternoon sun. Then for the first time since arriving at Johnnie's, the boy who was made of glass spoke. The sound of his voice reminded

Johnnie of the small wind chimes he used to see in Chinatown. Johnnie had always wanted one of them, but whenever he asked his father to buy one for him, he refused.

"What are they called?" the glass boy asked.

"You mean the skyscrapers?" Nick replied.

The glass boy repeated the word "skyscrapers" to himself softly, envisioning these giants, now apparently at rest, raising massive arms with huge flat pieces of stone or glass in their powerful hands and cleaning clouds or dirt or perhaps even the stars from the azure dome that covers the world. He smiled to think that his father might even be such a powerful creature, one who would scrape the sky clean of any impurities.

"That's the general term," Johnnie put in. "If you want each one's individual name, you'll be disappointed. Nowadays they're more like addresses: "555 California" or "One Market." But in the old days, they guys that made them put their own names on them proudly: the Phelan Building, the Flood Building, the Hearst Building. I guess these days the powers that be prefer to hide their names, like they do with their families behind gates. They probably think the rest of us are going to come after them someday and they want to be able to pretend they're not who they are."

"Can I visit them?" the glass boy asked.

"Don't worry," Nick said. "That's exactly where we are going, just as soon as the skipper gets everything ready. I'm just taking you by my place for a little while. We'll wait there for the car to come and take us downtown."

The three figures stood together in the fading light, the room seeming to float on that light above a hundred miles of earth and sea and sky. The first wisps of fog began to reach them, blowing down from the ridge behind them, the tattered fog that had followed Nick and the glass boy down the eastern slope of Twin Peaks and through the wet woods to Johnnie's house. It was beginning to descend swiftly down the same trail they had followed, blown through the woods that they had traversed, and had now come to lick at the walls of Johnnie's house, sniffing, seeking any gaps in the wooden structure.

Night fell.

*

Speeding through the same fading light that the trio was watching from Johnnie's house, a black town car ferried Billy and the rest of his crew into the midst of the glittering towers. The car rolled down the ramp into the garage below Billy's own SpinWare Tower.[*]

Louis had sprung from the car while it was still rolling and raced ahead of it. He chattered into his cell phone while hopping aboard an express elevator to the Executive Suite, going ahead to make sure that the various attendants in the Lounge and the kitchen and the Spa held their stations, ready for the arrival of Mr. Ferris and his entourage.

Billy's private elevator, at the door of which the black car finally came to a stop, waited with its wide doors open, its interior blood-red cherry paneling bathed in soft light from sconces of amber glass. The four mariners lifted their exhausted bodies from the soft, warm, yet temporary comfort of the car. They stood in the dimly lit box of cherry wood as it lifted them past the seventy-seven

---

[*] Here I must in all fairness note that while Billy's tower had been named for his corporation and not for himself, Billy's self-aggrandizement had not suffered in the least. Shortly after the building's completion, the Mayor and the Board of Supervisors had managed to rename the block of Water Street from which one entered the SpinWare Tower "Ferris Place". The official address of the gleaming cylindrical edifice therefore became "One Ferris Place".

84

floors on which thousands of workers spent their daily lives, arriving at last on the seventy-ninth floor.

Gus had had some idea what Billy's private fiefdom would be like, but both Marty and Joe were unprepared when the elevator doors opened. Hardwood floors thick with Persian carpets stretched before them to great walls of glass. They stepped out of the elevator and onto what might have been a platform of magic carpets hovering above The City.

An oversized fireplace, big enough for a man to stand in, held three giant limbs of oak ablaze, warming them through, truly warming them, for the first time since their boat had succumbed to the storm and the sea. A knot inside each man that had pulled tight when they had first felt the icy waters and had held fast for three days, now gave way. They wandered slowly forward, toward the heat and the open sky.

Billy led them past the fire and, turning to face them, extended his hand to shake each of theirs in turn, saying "Marty; Gus; Joe: you know how I have depended on you. What can I say? We never could have made it, any of us, if we had not all been together.

"I am grateful to you for all you have done

and for staying with me now. I know how anxious we all are to get home. But first, please, spend a little time relaxing with me. Let me show my appreciation before we go our separate ways.

"Please go on ahead into the Spa there on the left. They'll get you fixed up and comfortable. Then we can all meet in the dining room. I know you've all got to be as hungry as I am. But let's get cleaned up before we eat. Then dinner."

Billy lavished all the luxuries he could on his men. Hot showers were followed by massage, full-body herbal wraps, and finally a five-course dinner prepared by his personal chef. After dinner, he poured each of them a large glass of his finest brandy and settled them into over-stuffed chairs in front of yet another blazing fireplace, this one in the ante-room of his private offices.

Billy waited for the rest to nod off in those chairs, warmly wrapped in soft, thick robes from the spa. When he could see that Marty, the last to succumb, had finally fallen asleep, Billy Ferris tip-toed out and went straight to his desk. He got to work on the dozen phone calls he had planned during the previous three days, leaving his crew to snore.

*

Marty

"I couldn't resist working the Great Billy Ferris's nerves while he waited for us all to fall asleep. I would pretend I was slipping off and then just as he was getting ready to sneak off, I'd jerk myself awake. I loved seeing him get more and more annoyed each time. I was just pissed off at him for not letting us just go our own ways, get the hell home and sleep in our own beds, and instead he was taking us all prisoner, especially poor old Joe, but beyond that, I didn't trust him.

"Fact is, you just can't trust the rich. Even if someone gets their start with Daddy leaving them forty million -- like what happened to Ferris -- and they pretend they didn't do anything shady to get that rich -- didn't trample on anybody's life -- well, you just don't get as rich as Billy Ferris was without screwing somebody -- or a lot of somebodies -- along the way. So I wasn't sure what he had up his sleeve that night, but I knew that all his elaborate hospitality was not coming from his heart. Like everything else Ferris did, it was calculated for some purpose.

"As soon as it became clear that his plan was to start by knocking us all out, with the hot tub and sauna, the big dinner, and then the brandy, I decided to pour most of my drink in the fire when he wasn't looking and stay awake to keep an eye on him.

"I finally to give up the little game I was playing with him, pretending to nod off and the wake up again, since I realized that I wouldn't find out anything about his plans until he thought I really was asleep. So I faked it and waited for him to slip out of the room.

"I don't know why I wanted so bad to monkey-wrench Ferris's plan. Like I said, I resented the way he was pushing us all around -- basically like a boss who makes you stay chained to your desk all night -- but then again he wasn't doing anything more arrogant than was usual with him. Prior to this, I had never talked back or complained. Over a period of about five years leading up to that night, I had crewed for him a dozen times and, other than his appalling vulgarity -- I once even saw him piss over the side in full view of three other boats -- I found him no worse than the rest of his class. But for some reason, this time, I had to get in his way."

Six

Dusk lingered in the clear air over the bay, but on Johnnie's hillside the fog was closing in fast. The swift fall of darkness surprised Nick. He had grown comfortable at Johnnie's and had almost forgotten his original rationalization for disobeying the Captain's orders: Nick had intended to stay only long enough to allow him to conduct the boy of glass home under cover of darkness.

"Hey listen man," Nick said when the night and the fog had become so thick that he could not even see the house next to Johnnie's. "We gotta get going. The skipper will have my head if he calls and finds out that I haven't even got him to my place yet. I'm supposed to be there waiting for his call."

He looked toward the staircase but was too shy to begin walking toward it without some acknowledgement from Johnnie. The last thing he wanted to be was rude, considering all Johnnie had done. "Thanks for everything man," he continued after a few minutes, when Johnnie's silence had made him too nervous to remain silent himself. "But we really have to go."

89

Nick now looked to the glass boy, hoping that he might also acknowledge Johnnie's hospitality. He wondered whether he might have been mistaken in thinking that the glass boy understood everything that was going on, everything that was said.

Instead of moving, the boy remained completely still, gazing out over the towers downtown, massive blocks of darkness scattered throughout which lights were beginning to come on. He watched the buildings as they would disappear momentarily in the churning fog, only to be revealed again, briefly, when the constantly shifting wind opened a new hole in the fabric of mist.

"Hey, uh --" Nick began, having no idea what to say.

The boy of glass still did not move.

Johnnie, too, had remained still, standing beside the boy of glass. Now he put his hand on the boy's shoulder and spoke to him. "Thank you for coming to see me. I hope that I have been able to help in some way. Believe me, I'll do anything I can to help you on your way."

The boy of glass turned toward Johnnie and

nodded his shining head. He then looked up at Nick, who took that as a signal to get going. The boy followed Nick and Johnnie downstairs.

When they reached the bottom step, Johnnie quickly looked in on the young men in the back parlor. Nick saw him talking rapidly to them, and they immediately left by a door that led out to the side yard. Johnnie then rejoined Nick and the glass boy at the front door, where they stood waiting for him in order to say goodbye.

"Listen," Johnnie said. "You guys take care. Anything happens, Nicky, you know who to call, right?"

Nick gave Johnnie a sarcastic half-smile. "You bet, Johnnie. Of course I know who to call. I'll just --" Nick set about patting all the pockets in his clothing as he continued, "I'll just -- O yeah, but there's one little thing. -- I seem to have lost my cell when -- O yeah -- I almost drowned!" Nick said, then laughed out loud.

Johnnie laughed too, and then he reached into his pocket and pulled out a flip-phone. "Take this one, buddy. It's a spare. It doesn't have much time left on it, but it's enough if you need help."

91

Nick took the phone shyly, humbled by Johnnie's generosity.

"You know my number, right Nicky?" But before Nick could reply, Johnnie went on. "What the hell am I saying. Man, I am definitely getting too old for this information age shit. I forget that my number is programmed in the phone. It'll just say 'Douglass Street' in the contacts list and that'll be the house here. Just call me if anything comes up. I can always be there in no time at all."

Somewhere inside the house, another phone began to ring. "OK guys," Johnnie said. "I have to get that. Good luck getting home, and have a great night."

*

Marty
"I waited long enough for Ferris to get busy before I snuck around the corner and approached his office. I stopped just outside the door and listened.

"Ferris was the kind of guy who liked to pretend he was just like everybody else even while he lorded it over them: you know, those rich guys who insist that the 'free' market provides a level playing field. And then they're the ones who complain about 'radicals' stirring

up 'class warfare'.

"I remember reading one of those 'newsmaker' profiles about him in The Chronicle when he had first built the SpinWare Tower. He went on and on about how he had planned his office as a statement of his 'openness' with his employees. He went on about how his door wouldn't just 'never be closed' but he would have no door on his office in the first place. People loved it. And it did all sound pretty good -- at least till you thought about how many levels of security you had to get past to just get yourself on the same floor as his famously 'open' office.

"So I stood outside Billy's non-existent door to listen to what he was up to. I admit it. I'm not above taking advantage of a guy's foolishness once in a while, especially when he's taking advantage of other people all the time.

"I had thought that his first call might be to the Mayor, but protocol had given way to the practical. I should have expected it. His first call was to the reporter at The Chronicle who wrote that puff-piece I just mentioned. Her name is Julie Sands. She had spent three days aboard the Pride and Joy when she was working on it, two years before.

"'I thought,' Ferris was saying, 'that if anyone of these men had returned to his family and friends and told them of my discovery --" I mean, don't you love that? Here this kid saves his ass and Ferris thinks he owns

93

him. Then Ferris goes on and on about how 'We would have been mobbed. People would undoubtedly try to exploit the situation.' As if the son-of-a-bitch wasn't doing that himself. 'Some nut would want to make himself famous by shooting things up,' he said. 'Or some preacher would start carrying on about the Devil's work, or -- well, you know, the paparazzi are killers.'

"Then he added, 'I just want to keep everything quiet until all the facts can be laid out in an orderly and rational way. And I wanted to make sure that you, Julie, got wind of this before anyone else in the press. I admire you and like to think that I have been some help to you in your career. I like you, Julie, and, if I may say so, I am proud of you and your efforts to inform the public. I'm sure you'll set the right tone. I have full confidence in you, Julie.'

"God, the guy could lay it on thick. And of course they both knew perfectly well that she would get another big leg-up in her career with this story. Guys like Ferris, they're salesmen, really. Everybody calls them 'brilliant entrepreneurs' or 'innovators' but the fact is they're just the same as the old Fuller Brush man or the Mary Kay gal or -- better yet -- some door-to-door guy selling Bibles. A salesman takes care of his own interests by convincing others that their interests are the same as his. Or it's more like he manages to convince them that they have this or that need, which just happens to be to his benefit, and never gives them time to work out for themselves what their *own true interests are.*

"Never underestimate the happiness people feel when they are disburdened of responsibility for themselves.

"I must have stood in that hallway for about an hour, listening to Ferris work everyone, including the Mayor. I remember him referring to the Mayor once as 'that tree-hugging piss-ant', which was a totally illogical slur because the Mayor's political preoccupation was with poverty, not the environment. Maybe Ferris had a hard time telling the difference between people and plants.

"Anyway, he managed to sell the Mayor on having discovered some kind of avatar of the true nature of life, of humanity as part of nature, not 'man versus nature'. This discovery would help humanity to come into harmony with the eco-system. Old Billy came within spitting distance of some airy-fairy, quasi-astrological, quasi-metaphysical world in tune with the rhythms of the cosmos, riding the waves of karmic energy. But good old Billy always knew when he was laying it on too thick, and he rounded it all up into something pseudo-scientific -- or at least something that sounded adult and plausible.

"But I got tired pretty quick of listening to him weave his webs. I got fucking sick and tired. I almost fell asleep on my feet. So I quietly made my way back to join Gus and Joe, who were enjoying the first comfortable sleep any of us had had in three days.

"I didn't know what to do with the information I had gathered, but I knew that Ferris was planning a big press conference at 10:00 the next morning, and I knew that he planned to have the glass boy brought to the building well before that hour. I also knew that he had asked his contacts in Homeland Security not to interfere.

"He justified the last point on the grounds that the appearance of a lot of force among the crowded streets of the financial district would cause more problems that it might solve. He suggested that people would become alarmed at a show of force for no apparent reason. He even said that people would assume that the presence of Homeland Security meant a terrorist threat. I almost laughed out loud to hear him unknowingly get it so right.

"I fell asleep thinking about the show he was going to make of the glass boy, presenting him to the world. Ferris was setting himself up to be the maestro, conducting people and events in a stirring tribute to his own adventurous spirit when the asshole had in fact almost gotten all of us killed. I think he needed to show the world that he wasn't just a spoiled rich kid, which he was, but that he had some new vision of life that would benefit the world.

"I fell asleep and dreamed of a King who ruled over a floating island in the sky. This King plotted the capture of myriad fantastic creatures, many of them *shape-shifters, who surrounded his Kingdom. But each time he attempted to capture them, they simply melted through his fingers, or his nets, his traps, and his lassos, because they were, after all, clouds."*

*

As the glass boy followed Nick out into the night air, he inhaled deeply, and his shoulders relaxed. The smell of the sea in the moist night air calmed him. At home, his lungs had always been filled by moist and salty air. He had never before drawn a breath so dry, so void, as those he had drawn in Johnnie's house.

The glass boy had found his way inland largely by smell. He had sniffed out the direction of the driest breezes and walked away from the smell of the sea. He had wandered into increasingly empty air, but now the fog brought in a rush of moisture, and he missed his mother dearly.

The glass boy followed Nick down the steep streets. The fog swirled and thickened around them, making the light cast by streetlamps look like orange balls suspended above the asphalt, which had been turned a glossy black by the precipitation. Where the fog thinned from time to time, the skyscrapers downtown showed through with softened edges, their lights forming haloes around them in the glowing damp.

When the glass boy had first seen the towers from Twin Peaks, the late afternoon sun had struck them with glancing blows that flashed off their myriad windows in brilliant lines and planes. The dazzling reflections had made him think of The City as not unlike the crystals of salt he had seen in the rime that formed near the sea in winter or the pieces of quartz he occasionally found on the cliffs. But nothing in his experience had prepared him for the sight of the City lit from within.

Or, perhaps, not nothing: the boy of glass now understood the distant ships he had seen passing at night. He had always thought that they were tiny things which rode the waves with preternatural weight. Now the things that had seemed fantastic turned out to be marvelous: the ships had been, in fact, floating cities.

Walking through the darkened streets, walled in by houses that stood like low cliffs, was like swimming through a sea of light which rose higher here, or fell deeper there, along the shoals and reefs of buildings. Nick kept their path to the shadows as best he could, keeping to the edges of each streetlamp's puddle of light if he could not circumnavigate it entirely.

When a car would pass, he made sure the boy kept his head down.

They had walked about half the distance it would take to reach Nick's apartment, when the dim and quiet atmosphere through which they moved was rent by gunshots.

Panicked by the sudden sound, Nick forgot all caution and stopped directly beneath a bright streetlamp, looking all around them for the source of the gunfire. The handful of people who were also on that block -- two men just emerging from an Italian restaurant, another smoking outside a Laundromat, and a young couple walking toward them, hand in hand, from the far end of the block -- were all startled and stopped still, looking around for the direction from which the shots had sounded.

Two young men, both dressed in blue jeans and red hoodies and seeming like teenagers playing a game, darted around buildings and between cars, keeping to opposite corners of the intersection ahead and taking sporadic shots at one another. They moved in what seemed a nervous, jerky dance, not waiting to take good aim before firing and darting behind a wall or a car, as if it mattered not whether they had made a hit. Their obvious incompetence meant that neither was likely in danger, but it also alarmed the bystanders even more than they otherwise might have been.

Before the third shot had gone off, Nick had grabbed the glass boy by the arm and pulled him into the deep doorway of a hardware store. Simultaneously, he flipped open Johnnie's phone and made the call. In all, only four more shots were fired, separated by long intervals during which the young gunfighters danced on their separate corners like boxers waiting for the bell. Each seemed too timid to move into the open and risk exposure long enough to take aim at the other.

For about five minutes, none of the witnesses dared to move from the positions that had proved safe for them so far. Then one of the gunmen dared to run into the intersection, firing at the other, who had already begun running in the opposite direction and was almost a full block away.

At the moment the danger ended, the men leaving the restaurant and the man smoking in front of the laundromat looked at one another. Ordinarily, they would have averted their eyes from each other and gone their separate ways. Instead they smiled and shook their heads and began an animated conversation on the sidewalk.

The young couple, who had pressed together against a storefront when the shooting started, clung to one another for a moment, kissed, and then began walking quickly along the far side of the street, toward Nick and the boy of glass. As they drew opposite the storefront in which Nick sheltered the glass boy, a low, black, luxurious car, Johnnie's car, slid up, and its back door opened.

In the moment that Nick hurried the boy of glass from the shadows to the car, the couple glimpsed the glass face and stopped short. As the car door closed and the dark vehicle swam off into the fog, they resumed walking down the far side of the street, still hand in hand, but moving slowly now, each looking down at the pavement passing under their feet, silent. Later that night they would lie together side by side in bed, awake, each wondering whether the other would speak.

*

Joe
"The Captain had been gracious, taking us into his splendid home. Imagine a home that includes a private sauna, masseurs, and even a professional chef! My muscles had been so cold and had worked so hard that they were like knotted ropes, but they let go, in

the hot water and the massage, and my belly was finally satisfied by his beautiful dinner. Feeling so full and so warm, at last, I became relaxed, and my head grew very heavy when he left us to rest in his great leather chairs. The chairs tilted back so that you felt as if you were cupped in a hand of soft leather, the hand of a giant.

"Gus and Marty fell asleep right away, but I could not sleep. I felt so exhausted that I wanted to sleep, but I could not. I tried: I imitated sleep, as one does, hoping that she would mistake me for one of her own and take me with her to rest, but that night she abandoned me. I think I was afraid of sleep.

"I had almost been asleep on my feet as we journeyed home, dreaming constantly of my Siria. I worried over her. I knew that she could not have slept a single night since she heard that we were gone missing.

"And even before we were lost, I knew, she would not have slept. I don't think Siria ever slept when I went to sea. From the time I stepped into a boat until the time I stepped through the door of our apartment and embraced her again, she worried. And this time had been the time that all of her worries in the dark had come true.

"She would be kneeling, I knew, before the shrine she had set up in our entryway, with all the candles lit. Their light would flicker and dance over the photographs of our parents and our brothers and

102

sisters, of our wedding, of her country, the country we both love so much, but she would not see any of it. She would be in her mind with me, trying to find me in the confusion and darkness of a night at sea.

"There she would be grasping my arm, my leg, begging God for strength to hold on to me tightly enough never to let go, praying for strength to pull me back out of the shadows and into her bosom once more. She would pray God to hear her love and to prove her faith. So how could I sleep in that giant leather chair, full of a rich man's food, while she suffered so? I thank God that I could not.

"So I was fully awake when The Captain whispered in my ear, in the dark room where the others slept. He said that he wanted me to go to Nick's and bring back our friend. The Captain took me down in the elevator to the garage where the black car waited. He opened the door for me himself, and I got in. Then he walked around to the driver's window and spoke a few words to him. We drove off.

"Once again I was seated in soft leather, surrounded by rich wood paneling, with a bowl of fresh fruit at my elbow and fresh flowers in tiny vases hanging on the walls beside the doors. I leaned forward and knocked on the dark glass wall that separated me from the driver. It rolled down.

"I said, 'My friend, I would like to make just one quick stop on our way.'

103

"It broke my heart to hear his reply. 'Man,' he said, 'the boss told me that stopping anywhere was the one damn thing I cannot do!' His orders were to take me directly to Nick's and not to stop for any reason of any kind on the way. I could not ask the man to break his word for me, and so I told him that I understood, and he told me that he was sorry.

"I did understand, but it troubled me. I thought about how much my Siria distrusted the Captain, and I understood how she could feel that way. But he was the boss, and I had my orders.

"I sank back into the soft leather seat and looked out the window. Lights flashed along the streets and darkness opened down the alleys as we passed. I tried to think of a way to separate from the driver before actually reaching Nick's, if only for a few minutes, but I could think of no excuse.

"I could think of nothing. I watched as we slid along the dark streets. Sometimes I saw people leaving a bar or club or restaurant, or searching through garbage, but I realized that I could hear or smell nothing. It seemed that I wasn't part of the world, as if I had crossed over and was looking back at this world through these dark windows.

"My entire body grew cold. I told myself that I was just riding in a car from the SpinWare Tower to Nick's house. I had come to the tower with the

104

Captain and the rest, and now I was going to fetch the stranger from the beach, along with Nick, and bring both of them back with me.

"Then I tried to remember getting to the beach from the boat. I began to breathe very fast and even to tremble. I could not remember. I remembered the Captain pushing us on as the storm rose, proclaiming 'I've got it! I've got it!' and 'We're gonna whip all those sons-of-bitches!' and "I will win this thing! I will!"

"I remembered watching Nick working the starboard sheets. He would disappear whenever a wave blew over the deck, but he would still be there when I could see again. I looked at Marty, clinging to the foredeck. I saw his eyes full of hatred and his mouth clenched in rage.

"I had no memory of the boat sinking or breaking up. I could not remember the end of struggling against the water. I was in the storm, and then I was on the beach. I thought that the two were connected, but I remembered only the idea that I had been saved.

"I began to think that maybe I had gone down with the boat after all. I had thought I was back home, but still I was not back. I would not know that I was truly alive until I held Siria again.

"The car slowed and came to a stop in front of Nick's place. I opened my door and the driver said that he

would wait for me. "And that window," he said, indicating the one that separated him from his passengers, 'stays up this time. I realize that you haven't been on one of these errands before; so let me put it this way: the last thing I need is to see anything or hear anything that I might ever have to give testimony about, any time, any where. Got it?'

"I thought about those words as I got out of the car and went to Nick's door. I rang the bell, and Nick let me in."

*

Nick had been right in describing the first impression one had upon entering his apartment. The entire back wall of the small studio was glass, beyond which stretched a deep and full garden, deep green shadows shifting throughout, the orange urban light that seeped down between the surrounding buildings or leaked out of them settled like fine mist from overhead.

Johnnie and the glass boy were reclining in two oversized hammocks that Nick had strung between the trees in his garden. Nick had been sitting in a chair pulled up close to one of the two ceramic *chimineas* in which he built fires to warm the chill nights. The apartment was so small that for all intents and purposes, Nick lived in the garden.

106

Billy had called Nick less than five minutes before to tell him that Joe was on the way with the car to bring Nick and the boy of glass downtown. So when Nick opened the door, he said to Joe "All ready to go. We'll just be a second." But Joe grabbed his arm and stopped him from returning immediately to the garden.

"Nick. I have to see Siria. The Captain says that we can visit no one, but he means only to protect the boy, I am sure. It can do no harm to him if I go to my Siria, for just a moment, to save her from her fears and her sorrow. Please, Nick, please help me to --"

Nick did not wait for Joe to finish. "Anything! She's just over on York, right?"

"Yes," said Joe, "at twenty-second."

Nick grinned and spoke rapidly. "O man I've had this great idea I've wanted to try and never have. Come here," he said, now pulling Joe by his arm to the sliding door that opened into the garden, at the center of which grew a huge oak that reached over seventy feet into the night sky. "Think you can climb this oak, mate? Get out on that limb there and drop into the playground behind me there. It runs down the middle of the block all the way to

107

twenty-fourth. You can jump the fence and --
"

"I'm home," Joe said.

They had almost reached the tree when Nick gestured to the two figures lying the hammocks, swaying gently in the firelight. "We'll be waiting for you. Here's -- well, you know him -- and this is my friend Johnnie."

Joe had caught sight of Johnnie a moment before and had recognized him. They had never met, but Joe knew who Johnnie was. He had heard some things. He himself wanted to have children one day, perhaps a son, one day soon. Joe did not like what he had heard about Johnnie.

"Nick -- O my God -- why is he here?" Joe hissed at Nick's ear. "Nick -- you should never have invited him to meet our friend. The Captain is going to --"

"Joe, Joe," Nick said quietly, placing his arm over Joe's shoulder as they reached the tree. Nick felt the thick chords of muscle across Joe's shoulders, the massive trapezius and the deltoids like pompanos under his hand. He had trusted his life to his crewmate's capacity to grind the ropes through the wenches, as Joe had relied on him.

108

Joe looked at his feet.

"Now don't worry about anything, Joe. What the skipper don't know won't hurt him -- we've both already decided on that, right? Now go on. Get out of here. And give my best to your beautiful wife, my friend."

Joe pulled away from Nick and vaulted himself into the canopy of shadow, a green darkness shifting against darkness, into which he disappeared. Nick continued to the back of the garden, where Johnnie and the boy of glass lay in the hammocks.

As he approached, Johnnie called out, "What gives?"

"Listen," Nick answered in a low voice, after getting in close to the other two. "Joe lives just two and a half blocks away, and he's gotta see his wife. We just need to cover for him, if need be, which I don't think it will."

"Well then I can help out if it does, too. If Ferris's driver comes to the door, you and I will be talking in the kitchen. You go to the door and say that your neighbor, me, just dropped by and that you can't get the kid out until you can get rid of me. Say that Joe is keeping the kid hidden out back, but you can't

109

bring either of them through until you get me to stop talking and go home."

Johnnie watched to see that Nick understood his plan and then added, "You can keep him at the door and tell him I would be really suspicious and impossible to get rid of if I saw a uniformed chauffeur at your door. Make him get on back out to his car. He'll leave us alone till we're ready, and that'll be when Joe gets back. That simple. No one will suspect a thing."

Nick nodded in agreement but did not lift his eyes to Johnnie's. He kept looking down, instead, into the fire which he stirred slowly and at which glass boy had also been staring, as if hypnotized, all the while.

111

PART THREE

"Nel mezzo del cammin di nostra vita
mi ritrovai per una selva oscura,
ché la diritta via era smarrita."

Dante Alighieri, **Inferno**

Seven

The prayer of gratitude that flew from Siria's heart hung in the air as she embraced Joe in the entry hall of their apartment. But when Joe explained that he was not supposed to be there and that he could not stay, the warmth faded from Siria's face. She had never liked the Great Man Ferris. She had always resented his hold over her husband.

"That man brings you only trouble," she said. "and he is not worth the trouble you take for him."

"I work for him. I have to work for someone, and I make good money working for him," Joe said, his voice growing stern. But when he saw the hurt in her eyes he quickly added, "Money for us."

Siria leaned softly against him once again. "I know, I know, but to take such risks when --"

She had to stop herself. Her heart raced. She had thought that she would have had time to prepare to tell him and to prepare him to hear.

Siria took her husband's hand and held it to her belly. She looked into Joe's face, across which the flickering candlelight from the

114

shrine beside them played.

A prayer now flew from Joe's heart, and his smile brought tears to Siria's eyes. Then she giggled as shyly as she had when they first met. For a moment they forgot that time was fleeting and forgot the errand on which Joe had been sent. They were each absorbed in the other, as when they had first met in Mexico, Joe the foreign sailor passing a few days in San Jose del Cabo, Siria the student at the convent school near the Church on the town square. But time did pass, and Joe sighed heavily, drawing himself away from Siria's embrace.

"I still must go," he said, looking into her upturned face.

"I know, I know," Siria said, drying her face with the back of her hand. "But tell me that you will leave that man as soon as you can. You belong here, home, safe with me." She paused and then added slyly, "With us," resting her own hand where his had been, on her belly. "That man does not deserve you."

"I go not only for him," Joe said. "But for someone else, too, someone to whom I owe my life," he continued, regretting his words even as he heard them coming from his mouth.

115

Siria's face darkened with a question that he did not give her time to ask.

"I cannot tell you. I should not have mentioned it," he said.

"Should not have mentioned what? To your wife? To the one who carries your child? What would you have to hide from me? It must be something wrong. I pray that it is not a sin, and if it is, that it is not yours."

"O Siria, you don't understand. I am talking about someone who saved our lives in the storm. We were all drowning, and he pulled us to shore one by one. We all owe him our lives, I no less than the others. Our baby owes him the life of his father, and you the life of your husband."

Siria's face reddened, and her mouth drew tight across her teeth. She did not like to be told of debts she had not contracted herself.

"Now, now," Joe said, pulling her close to his chest again. "It was a miracle. He is himself is just a child. Don't be angry. Just let me go."

She had not softened while he held her, and she pulled back sharply at his last words.

116

"I'll be back as soon as I can," he said, bending to kiss her. She offered her cheek for the brief kiss, and said, "Or as soon as he -- or they -- will let you."

Her words stung Joe. He wanted to tell her that she knew nothing of the world of men and of the necessities men face. He wanted to tell her how hard it is to provide for a family without compromising your honor, to earn a living without losing your self-respect. He wanted to tell her that he struggled with demons at every turn, but he held back his words, his heart filled with bitter pride. Instead he told her of the long journey home through which he had struggled to reach her.

"I will be back as soon as I can," he said, pulling the door closed behind him. He left Siria standing where she had knelt when he arrived, in front of her shrine. She knelt once more, returning to her worry and her prayers.

Siria knew that she would not sleep. Joe's return had relieved her heart of a grievous weight, but his departure left new concerns on her mind. Recounting the things her husband had told her, she grew increasingly alarmed.

Siria kept hearing his word "miracle" repeat relentlessly in her mind. How could one child save five men from such a storm, a storm in which the waters had been turbulent enough to overpower a man as strong as her Joe.

She remembered the looks that the other girls had given her when they first saw such a big man meet her at the convent gates to walk her home after school, and how they had teased her about his size. Who could be capable not only of pulling Joe from the sea but of pulling four others as well?

Had the savior been perhaps an angel? The thought frightened Siria. It is one thing to pray for a miracle and quite another to find it answered in a way that violates the order of nature. Had her prayers invoked this thing? She shrank fearfully from the thought, for power like that endangers the soul. What would happen to you if you overthrew the order of nature to satisfy a foolish heart, or for vanity, or for a greedy, selfish love? Was this meant to be?

And if the stranger were holy, why would he need secrecy? To Siria secrecy meant dishonesty and lies, and she dare not think of the father of lies. And why would an angel come between a man and a woman joined in holy matrimony by the one true church?

Perhaps a power that could overcome such a

monstrous storm was itself monstrous and unholy. Perhaps some demon had entered their lives. Siria had always sensed that Captain Ferris had a shadowy soul. Had Joe been saved from a watery death by a force that wanted only to drown his soul? That force was apparently working even now to separate Joe from his beloved wife and unborn child. Who could the stranger be?

Siria remained on her knees, working and reworking her thoughts and her fears until she noticed the dawn light. She crossed herself and then rose to her feet, walking to the bathroom to prepare for the day that had already begun to seep under the front door and to stretch across the carpet toward her shrine. She would begin by going to early mass and, afterward, talking to Father Verre, telling him her husband's tale and asking his advice.

*

The same gray light that flowed in under Siria's door was stealing into the top five floors of the SpinWare Tower, reaching slowly into the inner hallways and the chambers that opened off of them. It fell across the desk of William Ferris III, brushing his temples, where his black hair had begun to give way to white. His head lay on his folded arms, resting on the desk.

The light went on into the inner hallways to find the lounge where Gus and Marty slept in the oversized leather chairs. The light pooled in the folds and valleys of the chair that Joe's body had left when he had risen just over an hour before.

Outside the light fell the length of the gleaming tower and splashed on the driveway. It flooded through the entrance to the garage as the long, black car returned with Nick, Joe, the glass boy, and, unknown to the driver, Johnnie, who was hidden in the trunk. Despite some anxious moments spent stalling the driver as they awaited Joe's return and distracting him as Johnnie slipped into the trunk, Nick had carried out his skipper's orders and felt certain of his reward.

*

Gus first became conscious of the dead taste on his tongue. Then he became aware of the stiffness in his knees and in the little muscles just above them, and finally of the orange-red light coming through his closed eyelids. He squeezed his eyes shut harder and extended his legs straight out from his chair, squeezing his thighs and his calves, too. Then he reached his arms over his head, grabbing at the air with first one hand then the other, extending them farther and farther above him, then lowered both to his sides. He let go of the breath he had been holding all this time, forcing the last of it from his lungs before he began to inhale slowly. Then Gus opened his eyes.

Sitting directly opposite him, where Joe had been when they were falling asleep, sat the glass boy. All the light of morning seemed to shine in his face, and Gus felt a yearning that ached. The boy of glass smiled back at him.

For a moment Gus thought that it might all have been a dream and that he was still dreaming. The scene to which he was awakening certainly felt unreal. Then he remembered Billy Ferris and Billy's plan to bring the boy secretly to his offices and to stage their return not as refugees from disaster but as triumphant adventurers. Remembering Billy Ferris, Gus felt his weary cynicism awake, and he knew that this was, indeed, reality.

Gus closed his eyes once more and drew a deep breath through his nostrils, trying to summon the energy to heave himself from the chair and begin another day. Listening to the last of his breath escaping his body, he also heard the thin, clinking sound he had heard on the trail home, which he had come to recognize as the glass boy's voice.

He had not been able to understand the boy's speech before. He had concentrated on it as best he could, but in the open air, with the sounds of the sea and the wind, with the calls of birds, the whispers of tall grass, and the rattling of the leaves on the trees, the voice had always been overwhelmed. Gus's eyes fully opened at last, and he leaned forward in his chair.

"What was that?" he asked the boy who was made of glass.

Gus did not hear the reply as much as he felt it move like a soft breeze over the hair on the back of his neck. "Where are we?" the boy asked.

Gus leapt to his feet fully awake. He held out his hand to the glass boy, who stood up and took it. Gus led him into the central hallway and on toward the staircase that took them up one flight to the eightieth floor, and into the South Ballroom, where they went to the great windows overlooking The City. They stood side by side, looking out on the neighboring buildings, which crowded together like trees in a dense wood, with staggered alleys between them affording glimpses of the shady distances.

In the dawn light the dim walls seemed less substantial than the honeycombs of brightly lit rooms within. Electric light, burning cold blue, revealed interiors shining through the windows. In one, a young woman in a blue dress laid out a tray of coffee and breads on a credenza which stood behind a massive desk whose cold leather chair sat empty, awaiting its proper occupant.

Out at sea, only a few miles from the luxurious tower, the warmth that came with dawn stirred a morning breeze. The rising sun touched the air, waking molecule after molecule, and, heated, the air danced, swirled, and then raced across the world, stirring up waves that it sent breaking on the shore, breaking and breaking.

*

"Joe thinks that he knows the way of the world, Father," Siria said to the young, dark-haired priest who had only recently come to work at the Mission and who was already her favorite.

"You say," replied Father Verre, "that William Ferris, as his employer, has ordered him to

123

guard this person, whoever he is --"

"Or whatever he is," Siria interrupted.

"-- whoever he is --" the young priest said, correcting her. For while Verre was indeed given to the belief that supernatural beings might appear in the modern world, it was difficult for him to believe that such revelation would come to men like William Ferris.

Siria kept her eyes downcast and moved her rosary through her fingers.

"-- and you worry because you think that your husband should be free to come home."

"Yes, Father."

"I understand your sadness, my child, and your indignation. But don't worry: your husband has to work overtime, and you should accept that fact. Let me suggest, however, that since you know where he works, you could visit him there, as long as you do not interfere with the performance of his duties."

Siria now raised her downcast eyes and looked into the eyes of Father Verre, which seemed exceptionally blue next to his black hair. She wondered at his goodness, too, this man who could assuage her heartache with his words.

"You said that your husband is at work. The person in question, the stranger, is probably with him Do you know where they are?"

"Joe told me that I should not worry about him any more because he would be safely on dry land in the SpinWare Tower." She pursed her lips at the memory of their conversation.

"Did you say something that you should not have said, something disrespectful to your husband?"

Siria's eyes widened, wondering how this young priest could know her so well. Shyly she said, "I told him that I did not think that being eighty stories in the air was safe on dry land."

Father Verre suppressed a laugh.

"Joe laughed too," Siria said, in sad acknowledgement that the priest, too, was but a man.

Father Verre put a hand on her shoulder.

"Wait here. I'll be right back. I'll go with you."

125

Father Verre then hurried into the church office and returned zipping up the windbreaker with which he had replaced his cassock, surplice, and stole.

"We can catch the J Church," he said, taking Siria by the arm and walking her out of the Mission and up Sixteenth Street toward the municipal railway line that would take them downtown.

*

Marty awoke alone. He had slept well, dreaming of the frustrated King grasping at clouds. He stretched and then stood up, wondering where the glass boy might be. Then he saw Joe returning from the men's room down the hall.

"I guess you guys let me sleep in, hunh? You sleep OK, Joe?"

"I didn't sleep. The Captain sent me to get Nick and our friend, and I only now got back."

"He's here?" asked Marty, suddenly alert. "Where's Gus?"

"I don't know," said Joe.

"But Nick and our friend are here, right?"

"Not only that," Joe answered, drawing close to Marty and speaking in a hushed voice. "The Captain does not know it, and Nick thinks that I do not know it, but Nick brought a friend of his along with us, too."

"So someone else has seen the kid already, without Ferris's approval. I like that. Who is this other witness?"

Joe's mouth tightened as he said, "A man called Johnnie. Nick says that he is a friend."

"But?" asked Marty.

Joe did not reply.

"Now come one, Joe. You obviously know something about this Johnnie that you're not telling. Level with me. Who is he?"

"I do not know the man myself, personally," Joe said.

"But you know him by reputation, is that right? I can see it in your face, Joe. OK. So you're not a gossip, and you don't repeat hearsay. That's honorable. But do me a favor, buddy: never play poker. You don't have the face for it."

"I do not gamble," said Joe, stiffly.

"No, I know you don't," said Marty. "But you do take risks. I have seen you in action, Joe. You have courage."

Marty put his arm around Joe's shoulder and began to walk him down the hall, away from Ferris's office, so that no one would hear what he had to say.

Eight

The rising sun warming the back of his head woke Billy Ferris from a deep but troubled sleep. He had not intended to fall asleep at his desk. A large and comfortable bed awaited him, always, in the small apartment behind his office. Few people knew that a side door next to his desk led to these private quarters, which had no other entry.

Billy had always taken pride in staying at work late into the night and getting to work early in the morning. He did so even after he had become successful beyond his own expectations.

When he held the first working meeting with the architects whom he had chosen to design the SpinWare Tower, he had instructed them to include this private apartment and to keep its existence secret. In fact, his belief that these architects could keep such secrets had determined his choice to work with them. He had it on good authority that they were already keeping many secrets on behalf of their clients, and he made sure that he knew a few secrets about them, too, just in case.

The tower complete, Billy delighted in emerging from his executive suite and

129

dropping in on his minions hours before they were actually obliged to be at work. He took a mischievous glee in the shock on their faces when they saw him checking up on them so early in the day. He knew that they had come to work long before dawn and had been assured by the security guards that Billy had not passed through the doors ahead of them. And he knew that his freshly showered and well-rested appearance proved that he had not slept at his desk or in an overstuffed armchair.

This morning, however, differed from any other he had known. The night before, after completing the last call on his list, he had leaned back from his desk to recollect the days since he had last sat there, on the eve of the sailing race that would end in disaster. He had meant to go over everything that had happened so that he could prepare remarks for the morning's press conference. He remembered the first two days of the race up the coast in his boat, the Pride and Joy, and even the first half of the third day. But Billy wearied as he tried to remember what exactly had happened in the storm. He fell asleep in his chair and was troubled by dreams through the night.

Billy had dreamt of a beautiful woman. Such a dream would not, ordinarily, have been troubling. At first they were swimming in the

130

lake on his father's estate in the wine country. Billy was himself, but he was also the little boy he once had been. The woman had been one of his father's girlfriends, between the wife who had been Billy's mother and the wife who would, eventually, be his father's widow.

Billy could not remember much of his real mother. When he thought of her, he thought of sweetness, not like sugar but like the sweetness of moonlight. The sweetness stopped his breath in his throat. He could not breathe. He could not remember her.

But he dreamt that he remembered her. He felt his body move through the water, closed in all round but also buoyed. As he swam, the strokes of his arms sliced the chill, resistant dimension in which he swam.

The woman was now Billy's mother but she was also his fiancé, and they had to get out of the water to dress for their wedding, Billy's first wedding. He felt an overwhelming anxiety that they would be late. He tried to tell her that they had to hurry, but she was floating blissfully on the surface of the lake. He looked at her there and loved her, her only, forever.

"Some things you can only get away with saying once," Billy thought, aware that he was dreaming.

He dreamed on.

Billy was struggling to get out of the water. He was dressed for the wedding, but he was still in the pool. The beautiful woman swimming beside him was naked. The bride stood beside the pool, beckoning to him to come ashore quickly. The tuxedo Billy wore, soaking in the lake, grew immensely heavy. The clothes sucked him down, the wool and silk and cotton, swollen with the weight of water, pulled him down.

Billy panicked and strove to return to the surface. His head broke above the water at last. He gasped for air in the midst of a horrific storm, the lake now an ocean raging and monstrous. The sea and the entire atmosphere above seemed to collapse on his head and again he fought to free himself from drowning. His head broke above the waves and he twisted his neck violently, shaking the ocean away from his face, salt spray flying.

He had lost everything. His crew was gone. His Pride and Joy shattered and sunken. Billy knew that it was time to die. But the judgment of the sea cast him out on the shore, where he lay, panting, shivering in his wet tuxedo.

Billy was wet and shaking with the chill as he awoke, soaking in his own sweat, at his desk. He remembered dreaming of a beautiful woman. But what about her had he dreamed? Why did he feel cold and sick to his stomach as he woke up?

Billy leaned forward and rested his head on his folded arms again. He closed his eyes and tried to remember the darkness of sleep so that he could remember his dream. For a moment he fell asleep again and dreamed that he was looking for a woman whom he had, perhaps, known.

Then Billy Ferris woke for a second time, feeling the warm sun on the back of his neck. When he opened his eyes, the sun burned them. That it should be so light meant that the day had begun already without him. Billy had to make an effort to pull his eyelids open. His lips stuck to his teeth as he tried to open his dry mouth.

Billy, who usually leapt to his feet the moment he awoke, remained in his chair. He found himself studying a large color photograph that stood on the desk before him. It was a picture of the Pride and Joy, riding high on a white crest, Billy at the helm, leaning into the sun as into the wind, his mouth open in a huge smile.

Billy held still, staring at the moment of happiness caught in the gilt frame. She was no more.

As he watched, her proud sails swelled in sunlight and her sleek hull lifted as if in joy, melted away, becoming blurs of color. The photograph receded into background as Billy eyes focused on the reflection on the surface of the glass that covered it. He recognized the shadow there, the dark silhouette of his own head. Studying the darkness, he began to see the features of his own face.

We never see ourselves for the first time. When we look into the mirror, we see what we have always seen. We pose. We draw or purse our lips, turn to one side and then the other, trying to catch ourselves off-guard, out of the corner of our eye. You long to know the impression you make on others. You want to see yourself without expectations -- to see yourself without seeing what you have always seen. You want to see yourself unprepared, as you really are.

*

Nick stood in the elevator, clenching his fists and urging it up the seventy-nine floors to his skipper's private suites faster and faster. He had become increasingly agitated during the twenty minutes he had spent with Johnnie in the basement garage. He had tried to tell Johnnie to lie low until 8:55 am, by which time so many accountants, admins, market researchers, and techies would be pouring into the building that he, Johnnie, could safely move around.

Nick had told Johnnie that he should go to the reception desk at 8:55 and ask to speak to the head of the PR department, in which Nick was officially employed, saying that he had heard from one of the missing sailors. But now Nick was grinding his teeth because he knew the folly of thinking he could tell Johnnie anything, especially what to do.

Even as Nick had been laying out his plan, Johnnie had kept on asking questions: where would everyone be, in what parts of the building, right now? Where would they take the glass boy? If and when Ferris met the press, in what room would he do so? If something happened, how would they get out? Which way would they run, and where would they meet up afterward, if it came to that?

Nick answered each question as best he could, with increasing impatience that he could not hide. Johnnie's mind dwelled on dangers and escapes, and Nick got away from him as quickly as he could. He left Johnnie in an unused corridor whose access to the building had been blocked off permanently in light of the increase in security concerns during the seven years since the Tower had first opened.

Nick hurried to rejoin the glass boy. He had told himself that he wanted to be there to protect the boy in case Johnnie caused trouble. Now, in the elevator, Nick found himself thinking only of the calm he would feel in the presence of the glass boy.

At last the elevator doors parted, and Nick saw the great man's private realm for the first time. He had not known what money could buy. Dark redwood walls rose from shining hardwood floors on which Kermanshah rugs floated like silken islands of indigo and scarlet, anchored by dark leather arm chairs next to which stood small round tables with brass lamps that had black, opaque shades.

Nick stopped short as he stepped from the elevator, uncertain which way to turn. He stood still and listened. As far as he could tell, no one else was on the floor at all. At first he thought that he might have gotten off the elevator on the wrong floor, but then he remembered that the private elevator had only one button.

Now that he had arrived at his destination, Nick felt the weariness of the previous three days settle into him again. The chairs tempted him to rest. He knew, however, that if he sat in one for even a minute, he might not get up for hours. He began to wander the floor, looking for anyone he might find.

The silence was thick enough that when Joe called out his name, Nick jumped. Joe and Marty both burst out laughing when they saw how startled Nick was. "Up to something we don't know about?" Marty asked with a grin.

"Not yet," Nick answered with a bravado meant to restore his own composure.

"Not yet? You mean you're not up to anything yet? Or we just don't know about it yet?"

"Well, Marty, that's a shock -- you mean you admit there's something you don't already know?"

Joe laughed. "Good one, Nick," he said. "And good to see you here at last, my friend."

None of the three had liked being separated over night. They were used to relying on one another in rough seas, when a sudden shift in the wind could swing the boom around and knock a man out cold and into the water, dead before his mates could make the turn to get back to him and retrieve the body, floating face-down in the cold sea. An awkward silence settled on them.

"Well if you're not yet up to something," Marty said, "we are."

"O?" said Nick, an eyebrow raised.

"Marty has an idea," said Joe. "If you do not mind making the Captain a little --." He could not decide whether the word should be "nervous" or "upset."

"Meshugga," said Marty, to finish the sentence.

Both Joe and Nick looked at Marty blankly.

"Wacko! Nuts!" Marty said, laughing. "It'll do him good, too. I believe I can say with confidence that if there is one thing the Great Billy Ferris needs, it is to be thrown off his high horse for once."

"Uh, OK," Nick said.

"Listen," Marty said, "even that storm did

nothing to humble the man. As soon as we were all ashore --" Marty's voice trailed off, and the three men stood together silently again. Then Marty gathered himself together and resumed.

"As soon as we were all safe again, the son of a bitch was right back issuing orders, and he hasn't stopped even now. He still thinks he can run our lives even after he almost killed us all. He's so full of himself he can't tell what's his to control -- if anything -- and what isn't. When we all know," Marty's mouth was tight and his tone bitter, "that it wasn't him who saved our asses that night."

"Yeah," Nick replied, "so?" His voice rose, and his brow lowered. "He is the boss, you know."

Marty's eyes narrowed. "Listen, Nick, don't go all soft on me here. You know as well as I do that Ferris is a spoiled brat --"

Nick said nothing.

"And believe me," Marty said quietly, almost to himself, "this 'little Georgie Minafer is gonna get his come-uppance'."

"OK -- so what the fuck does that mean?" Nick demanded loudly.

139

"Jesus, Nick," Marty said, "Somebody's gonna hear you -- and we don't need anybody knowing about this little conference we got going on here. Calm down, will ya? It's just a line from an old Orson Wells movie."

"OK. So? What's your point?" Nick asked. "We don't know your fancy-ass movies? Or we wouldn't all like to be spoiled rich kids and sail our own boats and give all the orders? Isn't that what you're doing right now?"

"Wait a minute," Joe said. "Wait a minute; wait a minute. Nick. Marty. Take a breath, my friends." Standing between them, he put a hand on each of their shoulders. "We have no fight with each other, please."

Marty and Nick looked away from each other.

"Sorry Nick," said Marty.

"Sorry Joe," said Nick. "Sorry Marty."

"That's better," Joe concluded.

Nick looked up. "OK, guys. So what's up?"

"Marty thinks," Joe began, "that the Captain has no right to keep our friend here if he does not wish to stay. We are still getting paid for our time here, but our friend should be free to go."

"Absolutely," Marty added. "Well said. He saved us, and now we may be able to save him."

Nick's shoulders began to rise up the back of his neck while Marty was speaking. "Save him? From --?"

"From the circus," Marty said. "You know as well as I do that Ferris hasn't got anything on his mind but Ferris -- ever. This time's no different. He may not be thinking about it this way consciously, but he's gonna turn this whole thing into King Kong, just wait and see. He's gonna be like Robert Armstrong --" here Nick and Joe looked blankly at him -- "Ok, Joe Black in the version you saw -- so Ferris will find some way to make himself more important and make more money and more and more and more of everything, all off of this guy who saved our lives. I think the kid deserves better than being displayed like some circus freak. I don't know about you, but I think the kid deserves some say in whether that happens or not."

So it was that the three fell in together, speaking softly amid the silken carpets and the dark wood walls. Marty went over his plan for Nick, and both Nick and Joe helped to refine it. "Little Billy Ferris," Marty thought to himself, "sure as hell is gonna get his come-uppance."

Nine

Father Verre helped Siria step up onto the streetcar and led her down the aisle. They positioned themselves in the middle of the articulated car, on the circle of flooring that pivoted when the train rounded a curve. The priest had calculated that since most people avoid the spot, they would be left alone. Siria clung to the hand rail behind her, trying to keep her footing and looking at the empty seats in the car behind.

As they rode downtown, Father Verre explained to Siria why he wanted to visit a certain friend of his on the way. The friend whom he wanted to visit was Reverend Pappas of the Greek Orthodox Church. He assured Siria that she need not worry about talking to a priest who was not part of the one true church. He and Pappas were very close friends, he told her, having attended the Graduate Theological Union together. Furthermore, Pappas had recently been assigned to the Chapel of Saint Nicholas which stood at One Ferris Place, at the base of the SpinWare Tower.

The Chapel, curiously enough, existed because of the SpinWare Tower. When Billy began quietly buying up the block of Water Street on which he planned to build his tower, the block which would later be renamed in his honor, the shipping business had only recently migrated to new container facilities across the bay. Much of the waterfront was boarded up, and real estate prices had collapsed.

The empty industrial structures, mostly terminals and warehouses, looked to the residents of The City to be dirty, grim, and quite probably unstable, and the people who still eked out a living among them looked to be dirty, poor, and quite probably criminal. So Billy calculated correctly that he would have little trouble getting the Board of Supervisors to approve his plan to raze an entire block and erect his gleaming tower. He anticipated smooth sailing all the way.

In fact, Billy later described the acquisition of the real estate, which took only seventeen weeks, as something akin to picking ripe fruit: it fell almost willingly into his open palm. Even the Seamen's Union, not a friend of the Ferris enterprises, could not hold out, and had to sell its century-old hall to the young entrepreneur. That particular piece of fruit, however, proved to harbor a worm that almost blighted the whole project.

The Union Hall had a meeting room of moderate size that had been sanctified as a chapel by the Greek Orthodox Church. The devout atheists who ran the Union had allowed this concession to their members' favorite opiate because the Church had in turn originally owned the ground on which the Union Hall was built. The Church had given the land to the Union at the request of its congregants, most of whom were members of both the Church and the Union, at a time when the Church, newly established on these shores, had itself lacked the resources to build on it.

Thus the sailors who made up both Church and Union could find their economic, educational, and spiritual needs met in one place. And the hierarchies of both Church and Union found that despite the disparity of their ideologies, their practices meshed quite smoothly.

Billy's gears, on the other hand, meshed with no one's. He tended to chew things up as he went along. And by the time he came to establish a presence on the waterfront, both the Union and the Church, their memberships declining, had reached such a sclerotic state that neither had the strength to fend off his purchase. Then, just as Billy was sinking his teeth into his project in earnest, he tasted that bitter worm.

A clever advocate in the office of the Metropolitan raised an obstacle that Billy had never considered and, if he had, would never have taken seriously: sanctimony. In the litigious weeks that followed the announcement of the pending sale of the Union Hall and the revelation to the public of Billy's plans, William Ferris III came to think of sanctimony as something akin to sovereignty, something belonging not only to people but to property. Indeed, he began to regard it, with great disdain, as something real, as in "real estate."

Billy's anger made him too impatient to wade through the legal arguments, but he took it that the constitutional limitation on the State's regulation of religion meant that one dumpy meeting room in a Union Hall could force him to negotiate not only with the holder of the deed to the land, i.e. the Union, but with the Church as well. The Church had sanctified a place and had thereby created a loophole in the 90% of the law that is possession.

Thus on a bright December morning, William Ferris III met with His Eminence Metropolitan Demetrios, who suggested that if Mr. Ferris could make room for a chapel in his project, and fund the operations thereof with a sufficient endowment of cash or securities, he might get his way. The Chapel need not be on the exact spot occupied by the beloved meeting room, but as long as it stood within the bounds of the block, the Church could manage to move the Holy Ground a little.

Billy, in fact, loved the idea. He foresaw a little jewel-case of stained-glass windows in a open iron-work frame standing just to one side of his great Tower. It would be a stunning piece of public art and a refutation to those who thought him merely a rapacious capitalist.

Whenever an idea took hold of Billy's imagination, he wanted to pursue its every detail. He thought that since he was an avid sailor himself, and that the Chapel was, after all, originally meant for the members of the Seamen's Union, that it should be named for the Patron Saint of Mariners. When he found out that said patron was none other than Saint Nicholas himself, Billy gleefully announced that the commercial mall planned for the lower floors of his Tower would be retail heaven, most pointedly at Christmas.

Billy reveled in his ability to find a "win-win" solution to any obstacles that stood in his way. And to his credit, the chapel, when completed, garnered universal acclaim from even the most hard-bitten doyens of architecture. The press took serious note of the young CEO from that time on. With the building of the Chapel of Saint Nicholas, Billy's celebrity began in earnest.

So it was into this little chapel at the base of Billy's monument that Siria hurriedly followed Father Verre. As she entered, she instinctively knelt and crossed herself, bowing her head quickly to the altar. Suddenly afraid that she perhaps should not have done so in this alien church, she rose quickly. As she stood, her eyes raced up the graceful lines of the iron framework into the vivid colors of the morning sunlight gushing through the glass of the dome above. The chapel appeared to be made entirely of light. The iron frame encompassed her like an elaborate birdcage in which thousands of glorious shards of light hung captive.

Siria gasped. For a moment she felt as if she had been lifted bodily into the air and left floating in the light that surrounded and embraced her. As her eyes sailed upward, they lifted her heart with them. Suspended in wonder, she looked around herself and began to notice the images portrayed in the light.

The azure dome, she saw, was not the glorious heavens that she had expected: it was, instead, the sea, as seen by someone beneath the waves. She was surrounded by windows that pictured God's creation under water: dolphins and sailfish, the manta ray and the shark, anemones and coral and endless strands of kelp that to her eyes, dazzled by the brightness of the light, seemed to sway gently in the ever-shifting water where they lived. Mariners who worshipped here could feel the grace of God in the ocean's depths. And those whose brothers and sons and husbands had been lost at sea could know here that they rested not in a cold and watery grave but in the very bosom of the Lord, surrounded by light.

Siria was still holding her breath, feeling herself sway in the currents around her, when she heard Father Verre's voice calling as if from somewhere far away, "Siria! Siria! This way!"

She turned around to see Father Verre and another man standing in a doorway just to the left of the pulpit. She hurried toward them. "I am so sorry, so sorry, Father," she said as she caught up with them, breathing heavily. "I was --"

"I know," said the other man. "It happens to everyone."

"Siria," said Father Verre, "this is Reverend Pappas."

"O yes, yes. Forgive me, Father Pa -- Reverend Pappas," Siria said.

"I am delighted that you appreciate our Chapel" said Pappas. Siria blushed. He put his hand gently on her shoulder and said, "I was just asking my old friend Father Verre to step through this door and into my study so that we may talk together. Please, come with me. This way."

The Reverend Pappas led Siria and Father Verre into his office, motioning for them to take the two chairs facing his desk while he moved behind it to sit. Father Verre turned immediately to Siria and asked her to tell the story. "I would only be repeating your words imperfectly," he said, seeing that she felt shy about speaking in front of two important churchmen. "Please tell Reverend Pappas what you told me."

Siria could recount her husband's tale only by relating her own. So her account began with the darkness in which she had been sitting surrounded by her fears, kneeling at her shrine. She told of her amazement at Joe's return, and then, at last, Siria embarked on his story of the shipwreck.

150

Pappas tried to concentrate on the woman's rambling narrative, but the presence of his old friend kept asserting itself in his mind. He looked up to see that Verre was watching his face intently, as if his reaction to the story and not the story itself were all that mattered.

Siria's own attention had wandered from the tale her lips recited. No longer thinking only of repeating her husband's words and remembering the sound of his voice in the shadowy hallway, she found that she saw swimming before her eyes the dazzling forms represented in the stained glass of the chapel through which she had just walked, and her voice trailed off to silence.

It took a full minute for Pappas to bring his own thoughts back to the present and to ask, "And then?"

"Joe said that a stranger had saved the five of them, one by one, from the storm."

"Yes, and --?"

"My Joe seemed troubled when he spoke about this person. He said that he owed this person his life and that this person was good and deserved Joe's help in return. But something darkened his brow when he spoke of this person, and when he told me that this savior was a child --"

Reverend Pappas, who had been nodding patiently as the woman spoke, now sat straight up and looked at her intently.

"You know, dear child, that sailors often love the telling of a tale as much as its truth, and in their stories, each may be stretched sometimes to enhance the other."

Now it was Siria's back that straightened as she dared to look the priest directly in the eye, saying, "My husband does not lie."

"O, of course not, of course not, my dear child. I did not mean --. I am sorry. Please, go on. Go on."

While Siria went on to tell how the stranger had come to The City with the returning sailors, Pappas thought of the stories told about the lost tribes along the coast. He had an interest in anthropology. Perhaps a member of one of those tribes might have survived, living alone in the wild, until now.

Then Siria reached the end of her, and her husband's, tale. "He said that one night, while they were making their way back to The City, the stranger had walked into the huge campfire they had built and stood in the flames and was not burned."

Until this moment, Pappas's narrowed eyes had given Verre the impression that he was trying to peer beyond the woman's words to some other meaning. Now, however, Pappas's eyes sprang open. He looked as though something had leapt out of the shadows into which he had been peering and had presented itself, rampant.

Siria was looking from one priest's face to the other, hoping for a sign that she had acquitted her duty with honor. Instead she saw that the two men's eyes were locked upon each other. Father Verre broke the silence.

"Thank you, Siria, for the concern and devotion you have shown in bringing this information directly to the Church. You have shown your awareness and your wisdom." Siria felt relieved of the burden her knowledge had become and of her fear of looking foolish in these men's eyes. Tears came to her eyes, and she slumped in her chair.

"There, there, dear child," Father Verre intoned. "You must be exhausted after all those days of fearing for your husband and these hours of worrying about this stranger."

"I can only imagine, Siria," said the Reverend Pappas, "what you have been through." He rose and came around the front of his desk, holding out his hand, motioning to her to rise from her chair and walk with him. "Let me take you to the Parish House across the street so that you can have something to eat and rest a bit. Then Father Verre and I will go with you to find your husband."

Siria allowed Pappas to support her arm as they walked, even leaning into him a bit, his strength feeling sweet in her weakness. He had mentioned going to find Joe, and the words reminded her of the nearness of Mr. Ferris. She gripped Pappas's arm a little more tightly. She would be glad to have the two holy men with her when she went into the lion's den.

They crossed the street to the Parish House, a tiny reminder of the neighborhood which had once thrived along the waterfront and which had succumbed at first to warehouses and shipping companies and now to the sleek towers that seemed to choke off the sunlight from the little people scurrying along the street. The sea-breezes, which still blew off the bay, sent a chill through Siria that left her shivering as she entered the building. As they entered, Pappas called to a fresh-faced young volunteer in a blue dress, who hurried toward them, slipping her arm in under Pappas's and taking his place at Siria's side as deftly as a relay runner taking the torch from her predecessor. She walked Siria down the hallway toward hot tea and a soft, over-stuffed sofa on which to rest.

Verre could no longer hold his tongue when Pappas returned. He began speaking immediately. "I didn't want to say anything until you heard her for yourself. I couldn't believe it either, at first," he said, though truth be told Verre's capacity for the suspension of disbelief was great and, as a priest, included the supernatural *de jure*. Perhaps he meant that it was harder for him to credit Siria's tale because of its source: he had always imagined that he would encounter the supernatural at first hand, not by word of mouth.

Pappas allowed that the story, while quite possibly not "true" in the strictest sense, was nevertheless "significant" and the source "credible".

"Although," Pappas said, "she may have lent too much credibility to her husband's tale, you must admit that she is obviously not lying." He remembered the look on her face as she told of the stranger in the fire. "She firmly and truly believes what she says."

"Yes, yes," said Father Verre. "I agree."

"So let us also admit," continued Reverend Pappas, "that this stranger does exist and that his nature, shall we say, will be of importance, perhaps being a member of the Lost Tribes, perhaps as something even more --"

"Miraculous?" ventured Verre. Then he added, "Tell me, Dimi, what about the detail of the fire?"

Pappas inhaled deeply and, at the end of a long exhalation, said, "There's the rub."

*

Johnnie knew how to get around inside all kinds of buildings. He had no need for Nick's plan. He knew enough. All he needed was to get behind Security, and the limo had gotten him that far. Now he could explore.

Johnnie had learned years before how to get in someplace to which he did not, officially, have authorized access. All he really had to do was to walk quickly, eyes intent on some nothing in the middle distance, as if lost in thought while doing his best to get somewhere he was supposed to be. He seemed to have always known never to use marked entries.

So Johnnie wandered through the mostly empty garage, ignoring the brightly colored arrows painted on the concrete walls, which pointed to elevators and stairwells. He eventually found a pair of sliding metal doors which, though unmarked, could only belong to an elevator. He found a small, almost unnoticeable button on the inner side of the right door jam and pushed it. Within moments the doors parted, revealing a large elevator car whose walls were hung with padded mats.

Johnnie immediately admired Ferris's willingness to spend the extra cash necessary to include in his building an unmarked freight elevator that would find only sporadic use. Johnnie had already seen a whole bank of freight elevators near a loading dock at the entrance to the garage. This one, he thought, must be designed for more discrete purposes. Somewhere in Ferris's kingdom, furniture and file boxes, and God knows what else, might appear and disappear as if by magic, independently of either the shipping and receiving or the mail departments -- and therefore of any audits. Anything, really anything, could come and go from the SpinWare World that hung high in the clouds above, without ever being seen.

Johnnie had found the best possible door. The elevators so clearly marked by the bright arrows rose only to the lobby, requiring their passengers to endure another set of Security desks and metal detectors, in order to reach the further banks of elevators that soared to the eighty floors above. Johnnie had found the only elevator meant to bypass the lobby and all security checkpoints within the building.

"Pay no attention," Johnnie thought, smiling to himself as he stepped into the elevator and began his ascent, "to the man behind the curtain." He was being pulled rapidly up into the atmosphere, the elevator's speed forcing his feet to press more firmly against the floor, not knowing where he might alight.

Johnnie had pressed the button for the seventy-seventh floor because it seemed just enough below the top floor, the eightieth, to avoid prominence and yet not far enough below to have fallen into the crowded world of the workers. A couple of floors below Ferris was too close for mere drones and likely to function more as a basement to the mansion than anything else.

When the elevator doors opened, Johnnie knew that he had chosen well. The air was heavy and laced with chlorine. He would find steam rooms and maybe a swimming pool here: he would not find a reception desk or security guards.

Johnnie ambled down the hallway. Passing an open laundry room, he grabbed a stack of clean white bath towels from the shelves beside the washer and dryer. Now he could be a guest or a new employee, whichever seemed more likely to be unfamiliar to anyone who might question him on the way. Johnnie felt the familiar pleasure of pride in his ability to master the unfamiliar and to make his way wherever he chose.

It had been a long time since Johnnie had been so young and so on-the-make that he had had to use these skills. He remembered that, when he was young and others marveled at his abilities, he would explain that the experience that had taught him these skills took place one night at the Opera House when he had been barely twenty.

It happened in the same year that he took the Art History course he had remembered a few hours earlier, in the presence of the glass boy. Johnnie had been waiting in the Art Department office to see his Professor when he overheard two other faculty members talking about the performance to be given that night at the Opera House by the woman

159

many called the greatest soprano of the age. Johnnie had never seen an opera. He did not know anyone who had.

In that moment, Johnnie had decided to hear the famous voice. He borrowed a tuxedo from a friend who had rented it to wear in a wedding the following day. He made his way to the opera house and found a loading bay open at the south side of the building, an empty truck backed up against it, waiting.

The driver of the truck and the stagehand who opened the bay door for him were gone but likely to return in a minute or two. Johnnie had quickly stepped through the bay door and walked with an air of purpose down the first corridor he saw, turning frequently and at random, until he was sure to be somewhere deep within the structure of the auditorium itself. All he had to do was to find a way upstairs to the rows of seats where the audience was gathering in expectation. It was at that moment that an officious woman had come around the corner walking straight toward him, a clipboard in the crook of her arm, followed by two men in dark suits.

Johnnie had maintained his deliberate pace, continuing to stare into space as if deep in thought. When he came within two feet of her, he shifted his eyes to look directly into hers, meeting her tentative question with a frank stare. She gave a little start, and in that moment Johnnie had seen confusion, a brief self-doubt, and was certain that she thought that fulfilling her duty to the two men in her charge was more important than stopping to question a man in a tuxedo whose presence, though unexpected, was also unremarkable.

Johnnie smiled at her politely as she passed and said "Good evening" to the two gentlemen who hurried to keep up with her, nodding his head in a slight bow to them as they passed. His smile broadened to one of great self-satisfaction as the three figures behind him disappeared down the hall.

Johnnie had then found an unmarked elevator that lifted him to a tiny anteroom backstage. No one questioned him as he strode confidently through a doorway leading from the backstage into a hall alongside the orchestra section, and Johnnie himself did not question the origins of his self-possession. The young man in the tuxedo took the lone empty seat in the eighth aisle, about a third of the way stage right from the center, and from that seat heard the most beautiful voice of his age. He lost himself in the music, which seemed to pour through him, the voice becoming his own, his breath keeping her rhythms as long as the music lasted.

161

Johnnie was proud to have taken for himself this seat in this sanctuary of high culture and in having taken it on the strength of his own wits and in the confidence of his own charm. Concentrating on his quest to hear the acclaimed singer, Johnnie forgot that he had been taught the skills he had just employed over a period that had lasted many years.

In the years since that encounter in the Opera House, Johnnie had told the story whenever someone asked him where he had gained his skill at subterfuge and subversion. He loved to say that it had all sprung from his determination to hear the famous soprano. The story, he felt, lent him an air of sophistication and provided evidence of his aristocratic nature, his quick wits, and the power of his charm.

Now, carrying his stack of towels and walking with the same charming arrogance that had served him so well all those years before, Johnnie strove to keep his mind focused on the task at hand. He was making his way through the SpinWare Tower, not the Opera House. The woman who had risen in his mind's eye had not stopped him all those years ago, nor could anyone hinder him now. So he continued through the labyrinthine corridors, thinking that it was already turning

162

out to be a good day, remembering, too, the voice he had heard sing long ago, and wondering what it was that he seemed to be forgetting.

PART FOUR

*". . . poor little talkative Christianity, and she knew
that all its divine words from "Let there be Light" to
"It is finished" only amounted to 'boum'."*

E.M. Forester, **A Passage to India**

Ten

Nick, too, felt that the day now dawning would be a good one for him, and he even went so far as to wish that all his remaining days could be like the one just beginning. He had passed into the realm of those who live well, the realm of comforting chairs, of soft, even light, and of redwood paneling so polished that you saw the life of the tree from which it was cut glowing in the whorls and ripples of the grain. He seemed to see himself, as one might when intoxicated, from outside himself, to watch himself moving through the rooms and hallways of luxury.

Nick's weight rolled on the balls of his feet. He sensed the rising and falling of his ribcage as he breathed, and he sensed the width of his shoulders as he passed through doorways. It had not been a dream. He had felt himself drowning and now felt himself alive, in his own flesh, and, miraculously, in these glorious surroundings. He had taken off his clothes and wrapped himself in a heavy terry-cloth robe, gleaming white, and was walking out of the locker-room at the spa when he almost collided with a man hurrying down the corridor carrying a stack of freshly laundered towels.

"Jesus!"

"What the --?"

Both men, startled, cursed and then straightened themselves up, only then recognizing one another.

"Jesus, Johnnie! You scared the shit out of me!" Nick said, giving the belt of his robe a tug to cinch it tightly again around his waist.

"Nickie!" Johnnie said. "What the hell happened to your clothes?"

"Man," Nick said, "this place is unbelievable. I mean, I knew the Skipper was rich, but you should see what he's got: five fucking floors of his own -- and that's at work, man, not even where he lives -- with a gym, a spa, and basically a restaurant that's always open with the chef always there. And not just a cook, man, a chef! I didn't even know there was a fucking difference before! Jesus, how rich do you have to be?"

Johnnie looked at his nineteen-year-old friend with a smile and a sigh. "Plenty," he said, looking down at the stack of towels he still held clutched in both arms.

When he looked up again, Johnnie asked, "So

what the hell is going on here?"

"O," Nick said with exaggerated non-chalance, "just taking a sauna and shower to prepare for my meeting with the press." Nick paused, and then looked into the eyes of his older friend.

"You know, Johnnie, three days ago, I was as good as dead. Now I'm right in the middle of all this, this --" and here Nick's arm rose and swept wide, his gesture magnified by the whiteness of the sleeve of his robe so that it seemed to take in not only the hall where they stood and the tiled room into which they looked but also, beyond, the entire floor around them, and the floors above and below them, and even the great world extending outward, on and on. Nick threw his head back and shouted, "And I am not fucking leaving this for anything!"

"Jesus, Nicky!" Johnnie said sternly, his tone hushed but nevertheless threatening.

Nick looked sheepishly back at Johnnie. "Sorry, Johnnie. I'll keep a lid on it."

"Hey, that's OK," Johnnie said more calmly. "You're not so careful, 'cause you don't have to be. You got a right to be here: I don't. I just don't want you to blow it for me. That's all."

"Alright, man. I get it," Nick said. "Hey, why don't you get rid of those towels and your clothes, and I'll get you a robe and you can hit the sauna too, alright?"

*

The white-robed Johnnie followed Nick into the spa, leaving his robe on a hook next to Nick's. As they entered the dark box of searing heat, Johnnie recognized one of the two men already sitting there as the one who had come through Nick's house, into the garden, and then disappeared into the big tree.

"Hey big guy," Nick said to Joe. "You beat me to it." Then he turned to the other man. "Hey Marty," he said.

Without so much as opening his eyes, Marty answered, "Hey Nick." He lay sprawled along the wooden bench, leaning into the corner.

"This here is my buddy Johnnie," Nick said proudly as Johnnie closed the door behind them.

The hot air pressing into Johnnie's skin and lungs left him short of breath.

"And Johnnie," Nick continued, gesturing to the other figures in the dimly lit sauna, "this is Marty and Joe and you'll have to meet Gus later 'cause he isn't here right now."

Johnnie remained standing, while Nick found space to sit on the small bench along the wall, squeezed between Joe and Marty. Johnnie stood close to the heater, keeping his head high in the hottest air in the room. His wiry body retained its taut posture, but gradually his weight shifted to rest equally on both feet, then spread out through his arches, rolling out to each side. His shoulders sagged a moment later, and Johnnie at last breathed deeply.

Johnnie looked at the three men sitting silently together. "So these are the lost guys everyone's been so anxious about," he thought. He felt small, his lean frame seeming to shrink alongside the muscular bodies of the other men.

It was the habit of Johnnie's mind to ruminate, always, on whatever opportunities it could find. Johnnie's thoughts moved naturally in a continual re-evaluation of his position, whether vis a vis other people or in regard to his physical surroundings. But at this moment Johnnie's mind seemed unable to focus clearly on anything.

Johnnie was aware how much stronger than he the other men were; then he was aware how intense the heat had become; then he was aware that he couldn't think how he should respond if one of the others became threatening; then he was aware of the heat again, and then of the bodies around him again, and then of the darkness and then of the smallness of the room they were in.

Sweat running off his forehead stung his eyes, and he kept trying to wipe it off with the back of his arm. Johnnie was blinking furiously. His eyes tearing up, he looked over at Nick, who, being nineteen, would be stronger than the forty-two year old Johnnie no matter what. But then there was Joe, who must have been in his mid-thirties, and yet had muscles that seemed as endlessly flexible as Nick's: broad planes of strength across both their chests, like the domed grasslands of the inland valleys, which would soon, in the coming winter, turn green. Their chests stretched off to distant arms, ranging like the foothills in the east. And there, in the corner, lay Marty, who had to be the same age as Johnnie, but who seemed to be made entirely of thick cords of rope woven into armor, the contours of which glistened in the shadowy heat, sweat collecting in the crevasses that ran along the fault-lines where skeins of muscle overlapped.

Marty's voice broke Johnnie's reverie.

"Well, well -- welcome, Johnnie," he said, "to the Private Heaven of William Ferris III." His voice, though hushed, had a bitter edge. "The Exclusive Personal Heaven, that is -- or maybe the Private Hell."

Perhaps the heat was making Johnnie a bit faint, for the words drifting up from the dark figure reclining in the corner seemed to swim about the room and redefine it, menacingly. For a moment Johnnie lost his balance and swayed dangerously, but he caught himself with an outstretched foot. Johnnie could not remember when he had last felt so out of control. He had certainly never experienced this kind of disequilibrium without having taken far too many drugs. Fear crept into his chest and began to climb the back of his neck.

"One thing I do know," Marty said quietly, "is that it is Purgatory for us."

"You know what Billy-boy's salary was last year?" Marty continued, now sounding more matter-of-fact. "Nineteen million, three hundred and eighty-one thousand, five hundred dollars. And that was just salary. The bulk of his compensation came in stock options and restricted shares. You know how many times his average drone's income that is? Five hundred and thirty one. He fucking pays himself five hundred and thirty one times what he pays the rest of us. So here we are struggling to expiate the sin of our poverty by enriching him who hath made us to work."

Listening to Marty, Johnnie felt his weight resting on his feet again, and began to rock slowly up and down on the balls of his feet.

"I have to confess," Marty said, "without making excuses or trying to argue anything, I've always thought that I was probably just a spoiled brat myself. Sure, I had all kinds of political arguments for despising Billy Ferris, but I felt like I was pinning it on this one guy in particular when he was just having fun and being successful and doing all the things that I probably wanted to do.

"But when we were out in that storm --." Marty fell silent, and Johnnie could see that he and Joe and Nick had all turned their eyes inward, seeking out deep and terrible memory.

Then Marty came back to himself, saying "Hell no! God damn it! He isn't successful. He isn't some better man, competent in some way that I'm not. Worse! Listen, Johnnie, Ferris is a god-damned idiot who takes chances that he has no business taking, and sure he's had a run of good luck in those risks paying off. But that motherfucker as good as killed everyone one of us on that boat, himself included, with his fucked-up crazy bullshit. 'I'm going to win because I will it! I create my own reality! I see myself winning and I win!' Fucking bullshit! Well this motherfucking storm is reality, Billy-boy, and it is completely out of your control. And we're all dead because of your stupid arrogant 'I-create-my-reality' bullshit!

"So Johnnie, I just want you to know that I hate that motherfucker for almost killing us all and for not even realizing it. We owe everything to the boy of glass, not to Billy Ferris, and you know what? I'll bet the asshole thinks he 'manifested' the kid in his hour of need. Fuck! Fuck Billy Ferris! And God help the glass boy!"

It took Marty a minute to catch his breath in the searing heat. When he did, he said, "So let me get to the point. We," here he looked quickly to Nick and Joe and then turned back to Johnnie, "we have our own little blow to strike for the rights of man -- any kind of man. We intend to keep the boy free. He will not become a trophy for Billy Ferris to add to his collection. He will not be trotted around the country, or the world, to further anyone else's agenda or ego."

Johnnie nodded, waiting to hear where this conspiracy was headed and hoping it would not run contrary to the various advantages to be had by attaching himself to the rich man under discussion.

"You know how it will go," Marty said. "They'll haul in all kinds of specialists and academics: anthropologists, linguists, physicists -- Jesus! If you think about it, they'll probably be secretly wishing he would die so that they could grind him up and feed him through some mass-spectrometer -- fuck!" Marty's lips pulled to a tight line, and he fell silent. Joe had looked up with sharp disapproval whenever Marty cursed.

"If we leave him with Ferris," Marty resumed, "all he will ever know is the world of money and possessions, of living as shopping. He'll never really learn about us -- about men, real men, about who we are, about humankind. All he will see is spoiled brats, materialistic spoiled brats."

Another silence settled on the room until Johnnie said, "Uh, yeah. So you were saying you had some kind of a plan?"

"There's a big news conference planned for 10:00, and I don't think there's a chance in hell of prying the kid loose before that. But when it's over, we're going to get him out of there."

"So you're planning to kidnap him?"

Joe looked alarmed at the word, and Nick blurted out, "Liberate him! Right, Marty?"

"What matters is what they're going to call it," said Johnnie. "They're going to call it kidnapping. Unless," he said turning to Marty, "you can make the case that it was Ferris who kidnapped him and you were only righting that wrong."

Marty smiled. "And a good lawyer could make that case. Unfortunately, he'd only get the chance after Billy's buddies had arrested us and we'd waited for months to go to trial."

"O I didn't mean a lawyer," Johnnie said. "You're screwed if you let it go that far. You have to control the terms from the very start. I was thinking more of a reporter than a lawyer. You need to hijack the press conference, not just the boy. Know anyone who'll be there?"

*

Sitting at his desk, Billy stared into the faint reflection of himself superimposed on the photograph of the Pride and Joy. He remembered the lurch in the stomach he felt when she would split a wave, riding up through it and dropping into the trough behind with a crash of exploding spray. He felt the wet wind and salt spray on his face again. Peering into the glass and seeing himself, faintly, with her, it seemed to him as if she had survived and he were the ghost. He felt the salt water on his cheeks and tasted it on his tongue. He was crying.

But William Ferris III could not go soft now. At least he could not be seen to. So Billy gave his head a little shake and took his eyes from the lost boat and away from his own dim reflection. He turned and walked away from it into his private apartment, where he at last stripped off his clothes and stood beneath a shower as hot as he could endure.

When he finished dressing, Billy Ferris called Louis into his office and asked him to draft remarks for him with which to open the press conference. Louis usually drafted all of Billy's speeches, which Billy then edited before delivering them. Billy had found that if he altered Louis's words enough, he also convinced himself that they were his own words, the expression of his own thoughts, and he delivered them with ease.

This bit of legerdemain had never bothered him before, but this time Billy had wanted to write the speech himself. He worried that Louis might not be up to the task. The delegation of responsibilities to others did not ordinarily diminish Billy's sense of control over things, but this morning Billy had a feeling that things were slipping from his grasp. He struggled to remember that night in the storm and on the distant beach, but memory seemed to run from his mind's grasp as sand through the fingers of his hand might have done, or like the brilliant inventions and insights that come to us in dreams and which, upon waking, we cannot quite recall.

As Billy tried to describe for Louis the furious storm and the terror of being pitched into the sea, Louis became aware of a change in Billy. When dictating the outline of his thoughts for a given speech, Billy usually rattled off a half-dozen incomplete yet overlapping "high concepts", along with a similar number of folksy anecdotes to illustrate them. This time, however, Billy was talking about his personal experiences in a way that was, simply, pointless.

Louis was also used to a certain condescending tone with which Billy would refer to himself, and Billy always had a purpose, usually manipulative, when he used

178

it. This time, Billy seemed to be getting lost in his own memory and to be forgetting the job at hand. Louis did the best he could to take notes as Billy rambled, but it was with considerable discomfort that he returned to his office to type out a speech which he would have to make up by himself.

*

Julie Sands found that five people had arrived at the SpinWare Press Room ahead of her. She knew all five. A local television news reporter who regularly covered the tech beat was standing with his segment producer against the far left wall. Louis, who Julie knew would play the M.C. for whatever show Billy had planned, stood to the right of the podium, talking to a cameraman who was just sloughing three weighty bags of equipment from his shoulders. He worked regularly with the aforementioned reporter. As Louis chatted with him, the cameraman worked at setting up his tripod.

Standing behind these two, and centered between them, stood one of the crew Julie remembered from her days aboard the Pride and Joy. He was Marty, the one who so nimbly sprung from one side of the foredeck to the other with the strength and precision of an acrobat arcing through thin air to catch hold of a railing and make an impossible landing surefooted.

Two years before, Julie had spent three days sailing with William Ferris III in preparation for writing a feature profile of the high-tech wizard. The assignment had come as a surprise to everyone. After all, Julie Sands was known to take reporting seriously. She had worked seriously at it and had long since graduated from such "human interest" or celebrity pieces to report hard news. Her editor had half-expected her to rail at him for offering her the piece, but to his astonishment she jumped at the opportunity.

Ms. Sands had, as they say, a nose for the news. On the one hand, she knew that Billy's exploits at sea would have no impact on the lives of anyone other than the yachtsmen with whom he competed and that his exploits were therefore not newsworthy. On the other hand, Julie knew that Mr. Ferris was already fast becoming one of the richest men in the country. Furthermore, she had observed that he conscientiously appeared at every one of the endless round of tiresome fundraisers and political meet-and-greets that gurgled and sputtered throughout the year. Julie sensed that he was ambitious for the further reaches of power. Though he had not yet made any overtly political moves, she saw that he was keeping his options open.

Ms. Sands had not met Mr. Ferris prior to her arrival on board the Pride and Joy, and her first half hour in his company precipitated numerous mutual pleasantries, behind which each was taking the other's measure. Having given sufficient time to acknowledging the formalities, Julie then began to unwind for Billy the thread of what would be the argument of her piece. Bit by bit, letting the business of sailing provide occasion for her to drop a remark here and a notion there, Julie began to give Billy the idea that his interest in -- no, his passion for -- sailing was not merely a rich man's idle pursuit but was rather a natural extension, even a celebration, of the much vaunted Ferris family's will power. The competitive zeal that he brought to racing at sea was one and the same with the much ambition that had made him such a success in business. She told Billy that the unavoidable fact of his wealth gave him influence, and this influential standing gave all of his activities, and even Billy himself, "gravitas." From the moment that word escaped her lips, Julie could get Billy to talk about anything.

During those three days at sea, Julie had also spent considerable time talking to each member of the crew. She had wanted to get at their feelings about the man for whom they worked, but they all knew better than to share such opinions with a reporter. They were all also reluctant to have much to do with her at all, since the presence of a woman on any vessel is, all sailors know, a bad omen all round.

Standing in the Press Room now, Julie Sands smiled at Marty. Ever since the first reports of the loss of contact with the Pride and Joy in the midst of the terrible storm, Julie had thought constantly of the four crewmen she had come to know during her time on board. She had admired their competence and their solidarity when she was with them, and it had seemed an enormous injustice that these hard-working and good-natured men might have lost their lives because Billy Ferris's unbridled ego took unnecessary risks in pursuit of a mere trophy.

During the days of uncertainty, Julie had pictured the men in her mind's eye, remembering each as clearly as she could. She tried to believe that she could will them back to safety with prayer. Sometimes she would concentrate on them so hard that she lost track of her surroundings, and then suddenly the newsroom or her apartment or the streetcar on which she commuted would rush into her consciousness and she would fear that her failure to hold them in her mind

182

firmly enough would mean that they be lost forever. She could not invoke their breath with the prayers she breathed to herself. Julie Sands would fall into anger at herself and into guilty despair at the failure of her prayers, the weakness of her faith.

So when the call from Ferris came, Julie had had to hold back tears. She had thanked God that they were all safe. Billy's voice became a mere hum, droning on in the earpiece of her phone, as her attention drifted to the men of his crew. When she caught herself and returned her focus to him, she realized that throughout the three days that her heart had ached to bring the four crewmen back safely, she had not thought at all about Billy. Whether this lacunae was caused by a sheer inability to think of Billy as ever endangered, ever losing control of most everything around him, or whether it grew instead from a darker feeling about the prospect of his death, she did not care to ask herself.

Looking at Marty now, she remembered what it was that she had been unable to remember about the men, the facet of their presence that she had failed to include in the picture of each that she had tried so hard to bring fully into being before her. She stood looking at Marty and realized that she had forgotten what it was to be looked at by him. She saw the man whom she always thought of as leaping and turning and hauling now standing still before her, gazing back at her with his dark brown eyes.

Marty, in fact, did not so much look at Julie, now or at any time since meeting her as she stepped aboard, as he watched her. Two years ago, he had watched her outsmart the Skipper with her flattery, and he had admired her for that. He had watched her use her questions to make her way into other people's lives, charming Joe and Nick, and even doughty old Gus, into telling her anything she wanted to know. He had watched her closely when she tried her craft on him, too, but had held back on principle despite wanting very much to tell her his soul's thoughts. He had watched her hair move in the wind, too, once especially when they we just off the Farralons, the red sunset burning into her windy hair from the endless horizon behind.

Since then, Marty had watched Julie's career from a distance, as her byline gained prominence. Now he watched her weave her way through the rows of chairs set up for the Press, making her way toward him. Julie's smile widened as she approached.

But in the moment that she reached him, Marty saw a shadow cross her face. Julie had become aware that her momentum was carrying her all the way to embracing Marty. She consciously had to stop herself. She held out an awkwardly formal hand. They shook hands, and she, again awkwardly, left her hand in his a bit too long.

"I have been thinking of you all the time these last three days, of all of you, and -- O -- and I couldn't think -- let myself think -- of being on that boat -- like I was when everything was fine -- but of being on it in that storm -- I couldn't let myself imagine --"

"Why would you?" Marty asked. "It was what it was. No one could imagine it; hell, I don't even think I could describe it -- and I was there."

Julie smiled as she said, "I am glad to see you. And I have never really meant precisely those words before."

Marty tried to think of something to say.

Julie continued. "And how are Nick and Gus and Joe? You look unfazed. Is everyone in such good shape?"

"We are all healthy and whole, yes. You'll see why soon. But before I say anything out of turn, let me just thank you for -- well, for remembering. It means a lot."

*

The boy who was made of glass became aware of Billy standing in the archway that opened from the South Ballroom onto the central hall. The boy turned to look at him. Billy immediately snapped into character and strode forward toward the glass boy and Gus, his hand extended to shake the boy's.

The boy shook hands with him, and Billy felt for the first time the boy's glass flesh, more fluid than his own, more dense, and more cold. Feeling that touch, Billy instinctively pulled back his hand, as if he had reached into someplace dark and touched a cold, slick muscularity, something coiled and moving, like a snake.

Billy stared blankly at the boy. Then, in the dark reflection of himself that stretched and curved over the glass boy's face, Billy saw something move behind him.

Billy's head shot round to look backward over his shoulder toward the hall through which he had come. Again he saw it. Something shifted suddenly from one side of the archway to the other.

Had it been a human form? It seemed to be upright as it moved, but Billy could not be sure. It was dark, the thing itself, and difficult to see. Billy shivered. He could not remember what he had been saying.

Billy turned back toward the glass boy and said, "Come with me."

Billy led the boy on a tour of the rest of the eightieth floor, which consisted of four ballrooms, each of them named for one of the principal points of the compass. Gus followed. They ended up back in the central hall, from which they ascended a spiral staircase to the top floor, the eighty-first, which itself had the height of two floors.

When they reached the top of the spiral staircase, they stood in the center of a single room that stretched forty-five feet in each direction, making a perfect square ninety feet long on every side. The walls were glass and extended from the bare hardwood floor to the ceiling on which floated painted clouds, just like the real clouds floating by them outside.

The boy ran to the north window and pressed himself against it. Gus and Billy heard the boy's glittering laughter and for a moment both men held their breath to hear it better. Turning to look at one another, they smiled at

187

each other, too.

The boy looked down on a small flock of clouds passing below and giggled again. Then he ran to the west wall and turned and sprinted the ninety foot length of the room to the east wall, running so fast that Gus for a moment feared that the boy would skid into the window and break through it. He did not.

The glass boy stopped short at the east window and gazed down. He had been running and laughing excitedly around the room and now he stood and stared down, silent. The boy of glass turned slowly around to look at Billy, extended his right arm toward the window behind him, and pointed downward to the ground eight hundred feet below.

"That," Billy said, when he got close enough to see what it was that the boy was pointing at, "is the Chapel of Saint Nicholas, the Patron Saint of Mariners."

The boy's shoulders sagged a bit, as if he were disappointed by the answer.

Billy suddenly brightened and said, "We can go see it right now, we can visit it, of course! It is open to everyone."

188

The boy turned his attention from the building below and looked back up at Billy, smiling.

Billy beamed back at him and continued his thought. "Yes, yes, you must see it. You must. It is really quite. I don't know why I hadn't thought of it. We'll go there until it is time for the press conference."

The glass boy looked at Billy.

"A press conference is a meeting, a --" Billy's right hand made small circles in the air, as if he were trying to whip up the words for his thought. "It's a group of people whom I would like you to meet. We can meet them after we visit the Chapel."

The glass boy walked with Billy down the spiral staircase, with Gus following two paces behind. When they reached the floor below they crossed the central hall to the elevator. Passing the archway through which Billy had approached them just a few minutes before, Gus noticed a small pool of water beside one of the arches, with what looked like bits of kelp lying sodden of the floor beside, but he said nothing.

*

Gus

"William Ferris III was a master of the art of handling. Captain Ferris could get folks to go where he wanted them to go, do what he wanted them to do, and they almost never realized that they were not acting of their own volition. His method was simple: he delighted people.

"I suppose it was in his blood. Certainly his grandfather had it, and I imagine it went back generation upon generation before him even. No doubt the famous Ferris 'will power' had developed through uncounted generations of schemers, each learning and adding something to the craft: flattering, cajoling, pleasing, moving people. Their obsequiousness doubtless never seemed a virtue until the right conditions came along: laissez-faire capitalism, a social milieu of sufficient fluidity to allow ambition to be thought a virtue rather than being recognized, as it always had been, as a vice.

"I have come to believe that no one ever did amass a great fortune without committing some major wrongs. No one gets that rich without dishonesty, manipulation, even exploitation, of many, many others. Certainly no great fortune is kept without injustice: a priori, to have is to withhold. So I watched Captain Ferris's treatment of the glass boy keenly, my observations sharpened by my skepticism, as I followed them down the stairs.

"I thought the boy of glass to be in particular danger

because he was himself without guile, so candid, so sincere. It was his nature to be open to everything and everyone, defenseless. It was even worse than that: he rushed toward everything, toward the unknown; he ran into the heart of the darkest unexplored territory. He was not just vulnerable: he literally threw himself into the fire, as you have heard. So I needed to keep a close eye on both of them. Yet even as an eye-witness, I am not sure I can tell you what went on that day."

Eleven

Gus

"I was following Captain Ferris as he led the boy to the chapel. We had taken the elevator to the garage level and then walked up the long concrete ramp that rises gradually to the chapel at ground level. At the end of the ramp stood the entrance to the chapel: a wall of glass ten feet high, with five glass doors, each of which pivoted on a central axis rather than being hinged at either side. The doors and the wall didn't actually reach the ceiling. They stopped only half way up to the sloping side of the great dome that enclosed everything. And even when the doors were shut, you could see the whole interior of the chapel, shafts of light falling through the stained-glass dome were made visible as they lit up the motes of dust in the interior air, floating bits of indigo, carmine, sapphire, and gold.

"And although the doors were shut, we could hear sounds from inside the church spilling over the top of them and into our ears: a phrase played on the organ; a loud voice calling; footsteps; the phrase on the organ repeated three times rapidly; another call; a door closing; a distant, metallic clatter made, perhaps, by cleaning equipment or metal chairs. Rich odors reached us too: a trace of perfume, perhaps, or the last wisps of incense from an earlier service.

"I could see that the sound of voices, worried Ferris.

He stood to one side of the doors, keeping the glass boy behind him, and asked me to go on ahead and find out who was inside. As I walked in, I heard the scraping of a chair and looked up to see the organist rising from his bench on the landing above. Without turning around, he went to a small door to one side of the keyboards and disappeared through it. No one else was there. I called back to Ferris, 'All clear.'

"I shouldn't have been surprised -- I really wasn't surprised -- but I was amazed to see how Ferris marched into that beautiful little church as if he owned it, seeming to be unmoved, even unaware of the passion, the soul even, in the great work of art that surrounded him. Ferris carried on about the artist whom he had commissioned to design the stained glass, about Saint Nicholas and the Seamen's Union and the Orthodox Church and His Eminence Metropolitan Demetrios, finishing his narrative at last with the coup de grace by which he, Ferris, had reconciled all parties and thereby made possible the great work of art at the center of which he now stood.

"Look, I had my day in the sun, my success, my importance, my money and social standing and even political power -- seems like a lifetime ago -- but I left all that. So even though I was once as wrapped up in myself and my own importance as Ferris was at that moment, I was still stunned to see him pontificating on the importance of the church as an extension of his own importance, talking over his shoulder to the glass boy, assuming, mistakenly as it turned out, that the

193

boy was trotting after him. He seemed oblivious to the fact that the boy lagged far behind. In fact, the boy had taken only one or two steps into the chapel before he stopped short and looked up, trembling.

"Actually, like the boy of glass, I was brought up short the moment I stepped into the space, engulfed by that brilliant dome. It literally took my breath away.

"Only someone with detailed knowledge of the materials used in making the glass, could begin to name the rich variety of colors in the dome. The first thing that hit you was the blue, the overwhelming blue, that surrounded you on all sides, like a clear sky at dusk, in winter. The color actually disoriented you, giving the feeling that the building that you thought you were entering had been rolled away, exposing you to the open sky.

"You found yourself tilting your head back to look straight up and seeing, at the zenith of the dome, the image of Christ Triumphant, commanding the heavens. Then you would notice that He wasn't sitting on a throne but standing, not just standing, but walking. And he was walking not on clouds but on foam, on the crests of endless waves far out at sea.

"When the glass boy first saw all this, he went weak in the knees. The Captain had just finished his speechifying and turned to see what kind of impression he had made on the boy when, as I mentioned, the boy staggered momentarily. I don't think that I had ever

seen fear on Ferris's face before, even when he damn well should have been afraid because he was taking risks at sea that he had no business taking. His face went white, and he hurried to the boy's side.

"When Ferris reached him, the glass boy, who stood swaying, as if he was dizzy, reached out and grabbed his sleeve. It was the gesture of a child, and it startled me. The boy was small, as I have said, and built like a regular nine or ten year-old boy, but I think that in the three days I had spent with him I had come to regard him more as a small adult than as a child. His astonishing strength and agility had made his physical presence feel more like that of a compact, wiry athlete -- a gymnast, maybe, or a master of martial arts. But in that moment, standing shakily on his thin legs, his head drooping over his chest, I saw that he was just a little boy, far from home, and overwhelmed by something he had seen.

"'Are you OK?' the Captain asked, gathering the boy's body in the crook of one arm and supporting him. 'Do you want to sit down?' he asked. Only then did he realize that the chapel had no pews or seats of any kind, it being the Orthodox custom to stand during services. He was casting his eyes all over the sanctuary, finally looking to me for help. All I could think to do was to help gently lowering the boy so that he could lie on the floor.

"I was on the other side of the glass boy, with one arm around his back. Ferris and I looked at each other

wondering how we could proceed, but after a few moments rest in our arms, the boy managed to right himself and stand on his own.

"Then he said to us, "Thank you, but I don't need -- ." He took a deep breath and then slowly exhaled, turning his head to look up and around at the dome surrounding us. "It is everywhere, all of it," he said. Then he closed his eyes and breathed deeply again.

"I lifted my eyes from the boy to look up at Ferris, wondering whether he understood what the boy said, but before I could say anything, I saw Louis striding toward us, officious as ever. True, he had not been able to resist the universal pull of the dome and had let his neck crane back to look at the Lord above but, being Louis, he did not break stride, not until he lowered his eyes again and saw the glass boy for the first time.

"I know that I can be a little snide when I talk about Louis sometimes, but I always did like him. Yes, I admit that I mocked his unctuousness. How could I help it? He embodied the kind of snobbery that you find among front-door servants. But I liked the man, all in all, and I was more saddened than irritated by his demeanor.

"So it actually made me grin to see Louis's face at that moment. His stern, clear-eyed positivism cracked and then melted away entirely from his face. His features softened, and I noticed for the first time how

large and soft -- and how blue -- his eyes were. When he reached us, he stopped and stood looking at the boy in silence.

"The Captain, accustomed to Louis's brisk efficiency, at first looked impatient. I noticed his lips pulled tight across his teeth. But turning toward Louis to speak to him, Ferris ended up looking at the boy of glass, too, and his face softened as well.

"Ferris was even smiling when he asked Louis, 'Everything ready?'

"The boss's voice snapped Louis out of his reverie. But he continued to stare at the glass boy as he answered Ferris, saying 'At the moment, Sir, I'm not sure what "ready" would be -- but, yes, the members of the press are all assembled and the broadcast technicians have established their uplinks.' He took a slow, deep breath and added, quietly, almost sadly, 'I guess we have to go.'

"Then the three of them turned from me and walked back toward the elevator that would in a few moments carry the boy who was made of glass to his first introduction to the world."

*

When Billy stepped to the podium, he looked out over the range of microphones that bristled like an unkempt hedge of thorns in front of him and smiled at the reporters, the cameras, and the lights, all gathered at his behest. For the first time in a long life of standing before microphones, Billy did not have that vague fear that something was about to go wrong and that he would be found out. For the first time he felt truly confident. All he really had to do was to step aside and to let the boy made of glass come forward.

Billy did recite the simple text that Louis had prepared. Hearing it coming from his lips, he knew that it was full of sentiment and empty of significance. He could see uncertainty on the reporters' faces growing, even starting to become alarm. Had William Ferris III lost his marbles? Had he called together the voices that usually trumpeted startling innovations or hailed daring adventures for some blather about a little boy? Perhaps he'd sustained a serious blow to the head or was suffering from some fever, or even an extremity of hunger, that would fog his judgment and disrupt his sense of balance.

Billy could see that such were their thoughts, and it made him happy to fail them, to disrupt their expectations. Then he took two steps to his left, and holding out his right arm toward the door to the green room, he said, "And now let me introduce him to you."

The uplinks from the vans were still working at that point, transmitting images and sounds of the events in the press room at the SpinWare Tower. These streams of data were the ore from which reporters and newsreaders were expected to weave, sometime before the daily news would air, a narrative or an explanation, a report. That data was, quite likely, all captured and stored at some point on its way, a snapshot taken of the varying shapes and intensities of waves expanding ever-outward to the ether, and perhaps one day they will be seen again.

As for those in the press room that day, none remembered with any certainty what effect seeing the boy of glass had had on them. The camera men had stared at their monitors and, at first, cursed their equipment for apparently failing at the crucial moment. Then they looked up over their lenses and LCD screens at the boy himself, and they kept looking, careless of what their equipment might be capturing. So too with the soundmen, whose huge earphones, settled on their heads like the eyes of giant flies, had seemed at first to betray them. But when they took off the earphones, they heard the same sounds of the boy's delicate voice in their own ears.

Those stationed in the vans, monitoring the feed as it moved from cables on land to the

199

dishes that sent it airborne, tried frantically to fix the non-existent problem with the image on their screens. They could not read what they saw: light eddied and swirled, light reflected and refracted, light shattered and reformed. Soon they gave up and sat dumbfounded, their eyes trying to pierce the confusion, to piece together familiar shapes out of the chaos of light, but to no avail.

They could not understand what they saw, nor could they ignore it. Staring into it, they began after a while to see their own reflections on the surface of the screens through which they had been trying to peer. They began to see themselves, and then to see the interiors of the vans in which they sat.

Then the images, jumbled and disjointed as they were, suddenly leapt, as if a great shock had gone through the world, and flashed, and the screens all went dark: the signal from the SpinWare Tower had broken off, and those who had been watching could see in their screens only themselves and the world behind.

*

Johnnie had proved as good as his word. He had indeed been able to locate and identify the switching apparatus necessary to cut the power to the press room and, in fact, the entire floor. Marty had positioned himself near enough to Julie in the minutes before the blackout to be able to speak quietly into her ear in the moment all went dark. He put a hand on her shoulder gently so as not to frighten her. "I will show you the way out of here. Turn slightly to your left and walk carefully straight ahead. I will steer you, but the way should be clear. I sighted it out just before the lights went down, and I expect everyone else will freeze in place rather than take any chances in this dark."

Julie would certainly not have ventured a step without Marty's guidance. The darkness was complete here in the center of the building. Marty guided her directly to the doorway that led to the green-room and then to the bank of elevators beyond it. So completely did Julie focus on stepping carefully through the thick darkness that they were in the elevator before she thought to ask where they were going.

"An exclusive," Marty said. "You and the glass boy. Private interview, one on one, ask anything you like. You will meet him in about two and a half minutes."

Julie let a sly smile spread across her face. She looked at Marty and shook her head slowly.

*

Nick

"Johnnie hit those lights at the exact perfect moment. I knew my man would come through. I stepped up behind the boy, grabbed his shoulder with my right hand, and told him that I would lead him out of the dark. I had him out the door, down the elevator, and down to the chapel in no time. I beat Marty and Johnnie and Joe. Those two hadn't even made it back from the electrical room and it was just down in the garage."

*

Julie Sands had covered the dedication ceremonies at the chapel She thought that she knew the place. She had read the statements made by the architect and the artist who designed the windows and so knew their intention to represent marine ecosystems. She had read up on Saint Nicholas, too: the legend that he raised from the dead three children who had drowned in a vat of brine; the iconography associated with him of three children in a tub, or three golden balls and a book, or three bags of money; and the position he held as Patron Saint both of Sailors and of Children. She knew that it was this latter position that had evolved into his identification with Santa Claus.

On arriving for the dedication, Julie had looked up at the dome as she entered, marveling at the richness of its colors and noting the figure of Christ at its zenith. But she would not let herself be pulled into gazing at its beauty and forgetting her work. She had pulled her eyes back down to the crowd milling about within the chapel and focused on the appearance and the status of the people instead.

But as she entered the quiet chapel this time, she began to see where she was. She and Marty entered the church together, and each stopped still just a few steps inside, first looking up and then slowly looking all around.

Where they entered, they found the low interior walls depicted fields of sea grass waving in the ocean's currents. Anchored to the rocks were Red-Beard Sponges and mussels which, being stained glass, seemed encrusted with jewel-barnacles. Where the curve of the dome came near the top of the door through which they entered, a Bat Ray flew overhead, almost grazing their hair. This lower edge of the dome showed a light blue like the light one sees on the bottom of a swimming pool, light moving in pale patterns, the shadows cast by the waves on the surface. These patterns of light shifted over the delicate sea-anemone, the sea-horse and the sea-urchin, and the horseshoe crab.

As Julie and Marty moved slowly toward the center of the church, they seemed to be walking off the edge of the continental shelf. The rocks and grasses, and the creatures that live among them, fell away on both sides and the blue overhead intensified, becoming a cerulean night that seemed to hang over the center of the dome. Nearing the crossing of the transept and nave, under the deep blue at the center, the interior walls darkened too, and a Tiger Shark passed them, swimming toward a Loggerhead Turtle. Hammerheads swooped above, attended by their Barber Fish, and in the distances whirled great clouds of plankton. A huge Sperm Whale also wheeled overhead, then turned to dive back down through the watery sky.

Waiting for them at the center of the chapel stood Nick and the boy of glass. The sun had risen high enough to shine directly down between the canyon walls of The City's financial district. Light blazed through the deep blue center of the dome. The air inside the church seemed itself to catch fire, inflamed with a million colors.

As they approached, Nick called out, "Hey Julie! Good to see you! I don't know if you remember me, but I'm --"

"Nick," Julie said. "Of course I remember you. I've been thinking a lot about you, about all of you, these past few days. How could I forget?" Julie shook Nick's proffered hand, and she at last came face to face with the glass boy.

Julie started to say "Hello," but she fell silent before the word could come.

Most of us have the experience, from time to time, of being ourselves and, at the same time, observing ourselves be. Most often during great emotional duress, such as in a sudden, disastrous accident, we seem to stand somewhere outside of ourselves or hover just overhead, and watch ourselves do what we do. Julie had always had an almost preternatural talent for both being and observing simultaneously: it was one of the reasons she was such a good reporter.

Ordinarily, Julie could interact with those around her quite normally, putting them at ease and getting them to drop their guard, while at the same time noticing hundreds of details and committing them to memory, making mental notes, as it were. She could hold in her head people, their gestures, their words, and the sights and sounds and smells of their surroundings, and write about it all

205

later. But looking into the glass boy's face, Julie experienced something she had never known before.

Julie knew the questions that a reporter should ask, the questions she had asked so often that they had become instinctive forms of casual conversation: who? what? where? when? how? Julie had not had to think about her questions or develop tactics for years. She had lost all self-consciousness about her job.

But in the weird light of this church, looking at -- at what, really? -- Julie was bewildered. She felt as if she had walked into a room and forgotten why. What was she supposed to be looking for? Wasn't she supposed to be looking for something?

She looked into the glass boy's face and everything around him faded into a generalized glow, as when you stare at a figure in a spotlight on a partially darkened stage, his shining form the only thing in your field of vision. She shook her head slightly and made the effort to focus on the business at hand. She intended to ask the boy of glass where he was from, but when Julie opened her mouth, she heard herself say, "How are you? I mean -- are you OK?"

The boy of glass looked down at his feet.

Then for the first time Julie heard his soft yet brittle voice, but she could not make out what it was that he said.

Instead she heard the glass boy's words tumble out of him like wind rushing through a huge, many-tiered chandelier hung with hundreds and hundreds of crystal pendants, a delicate and frighteningly fragile sound, his tale buried somewhere within.

Julie's throat went dry. When she finally spoke, Julie heard herself say simply, "Can I help? Is there anything I can do?"

The boy smiled broadly. He looked up at the dome surrounding them, and this time Julie caught the last part of what he said: "-- I mean, my father's house."

As the glass boy uttered those words, the little group of three people who had been hurrying toward them stopped short. Father Verre and Reverend Pappas looked stunned, and Siria let out a little gasp, crossing herself hurriedly at the same time.

Julie, her back to them, had not noticed their arrival and continued talking to the boy, saying gently, "But this is a church, not a house. No one lives here."

"There are many among us who might argue that point," said Reverend Pappas from so close behind Julie that she, still unaware that anyone had joined them, jumped as if bitten. The blood went from her face and then flooded back in, and she turned to look at Pappas blushing.

Pappas begged her forgiveness and assured her that he had thought she knew he was there. Julie kept her silence, but the muscles on either side of her jaw worked furiously. Reverend Pappas closed in on the glass boy, smiling and holding his hands together in front of him.

"Welcome," he said smoothly, catching himself at the last instant from adding his customary "my son."

"I am Dmitri Pappas, the Pastor of St. Nicholas. I heard your remark just now. May I ask who, exactly, is your father?"

*

Marty
"I saw the priests exchange looks, and I figured they must be up to no good. When Pappas started to try to grill the kid, I figured they were heading down either the Blasphemer or the 'My-Name-Is-Legion' route, trying to make him either claim to be divine or admit

somehow that he was a demon. I was determined to get between the clergy and the boy when to my surprise, Siria did it for me.

"She had tears in her eyes as she went up to the kid and placed her hand on the side of his face, stroking him gently. 'Ay, mijo,' she said.'

"Then Pappas turned to Verre and jerked his head toward the side door. Verre took the hint and quickly bundled Siria in his arms and practically pulled her out of the chapel. As they were leaving, I saw Verre looking over his shoulder at Pappas, as if he was sorry that he was going to miss the show -- or the fight or whatever."

Twelve

As Johnnie and Joe approached the chapel, the sound of Johnnie's laughter preceded them, interrupting Pappas's attempt to question the glass boy. In his exuberance, Johnnie flung the doors inward. His laughter stopped short. Johnnie fell as silent as the reverential Joe.

Overwhelmed by the chapel's magnificence, Johnnie could hardly distinguish between the stained glass figures and the real people standing right ahead of him. They seemed to form a *tableau vivant*, perhaps representing a scene in some sacred story. At the center of the crossing stood the boy of glass, looking at Julie Sands, who stood a foot in front of him. To the left, a priest leaned inward as though trying to get around Julie to reach the glass boy. On the right stood Nick and Marty, who were facing Johnnie and Joe.

Nick's eyes locked on Johnnie's, and he opened his mouth to call out to him, but before the words could emerge, a cavernous rumble, like thunder emerging from deep granite, overwhelmed their hearing. Then it threw them all to the ground.

*

Joe

"I thought that I must have tripped on a step I hadn't seen. I stumbled forward trying to catch myself on my right foot, but as my foot came down, the floor rose up to slap it. I went sprawling backward and hit the ground. But as I lay there, I somehow kept moving. Then I realized what it was.

"I braced myself, called to God, and rolled over so as not to be looking up, expecting the whole dome to become glass knives raining down at any moment. My vision blurred, and all I could make out were colors -- in all directions, swimming, shifting, but, I realized after a few moments, not falling, not falling.

"The ground beneath me heaved again, and I was tossed into the air and got slammed down on my back. The dome still held above. I lay still, and at last the ground was still, too. I wondered how long it had really lasted. Then I heard screaming. It was me. I was crying out "Siria! Siria!"

*

Gus

"As soon as I was left alone, while the others went to the press conference, I climbed as quickly as I could up to the organ loft in the southeast corner of the crossing. Shaped something like a slice of pie, it consisted of a wedge of blue ceramic flooring that was suspended about seven feet off the ground and about three feet below the top edge of the interior walls.

211

"On this floor stood the pipes of the organ, arranged along the curve of the dome, with the keyboards and pedals in front of them. In the pointed corner of this pie piece was the organ master's bench, with its back to the chapel. I immediately sat down, facing the grand array of stops and registers, the five keyboards, and the enormous pedals.

"It reminded me of the helm of a great ship, the organist like a captain facing a curved window overlooking the foredeck. But instead of looking out at the waters that lay ahead, this captain looked into a forest of pipes; rectangular pipes of polished wood and round pipes of brass, in which the chapel behind would show as bands of brilliant reflected colors.

"I wanted to play. I knew that I had time before the others would return, but my fear got the better of me. I told myself instead that I would wait and remain behind when everything was through, so that I could run my fingers over those keys and feel the grand chords vibrate in my body. That's why I never got the chance. I don't think there's anything in my life that I regret more.

"And that's how it happened that I was perched up there with a view of everything when the quake hit. I saw everyone where they were thrown -- saw it all down to the smallest detail.

"There are moments, when you get adrenaline rushing

into your blood, when you are suddenly on extreme alert: out of nowhere a kid on a bicycle shoots into the intersection in front of your car, and you know you can't possibly stop in time. You see every detail in stretched-out slowness so that you can take it all in: his body lifts from his bike and glides through the air in a horizontal pose, as if he were reclining on an invisible magic carpet, ready to sleep, but then he begins spinning as he rises over the hood of your car and tumbles leisurely into your windshield, which becomes a spider web of white cracks bulging in toward you, glass that shatters and bends but does not break.

"Or the moment when the field you are looking at across the road seems to flare up like green-burning coals, all the life in the swaying grasses burning with green fire in the sunlight, and the field itself hovering in the air just above the surface of the earth, and rising from it the four blackbirds, black as nothing, like holes in the fabric of being, and you understand that the fallen friend you hold in your arms is dead.

"So here is what I saw. As Julie was talking to the boy, standing very close to him, he inexplicably dropped to the floor and lay on his side. He reached up for Julie as if to pull her down with him, but she pulled back a bit before she joined him on the floor, where she sat cross-legged instead of lying beside him as he still seemed desperately to want her to do. But she had hesitated, and in that moment the subterranean roaring and the first jolt hit us, and everyone was thrown to the floor.

213

"The boy of glass must have known that the earthquake was coming. I have heard that in the minutes before an earthquake, animals in zoos will congregate each with their kind, the zebras huddling in one corner of their field, giraffes in another, the great cats circling in close together, and even the birds settling in flocks on one or two trees. He must have had such knowledge.

"When the floor beneath me stopped heaving, I grabbed the top edge of the interior wall and pulled myself up, peering down at the scene below. The boy made of glass lay in a fetal position on the floor, Julie sitting beside him in tears. I was crying too. I felt dead inside.

"I got to my feet and ran down the stairs to the main floor. Marty was helping the priest get to his feet as I got there. I heard Julie saying to the boy of glass, 'Shhh,' stroking the side of his head gently, 'Everything's going to be all right; everything's going to be OK.'

"Then I heard the most horrible sound I have ever heard in my life, a horrific wailing that split the air. It was Joe crying out for Siria. Nick and Marty looked at Joe, and the three of them ran to the end of the north transept, crashing through the doors into blinding the sunlight beyond."

*

Nick

"I swear I thought somebody had come up behind me and fucking picked me up by the collar, man. I mean, I apologize for the language, but there's no other way to tell what it's like. I got literally tossed about four feet into the air. It felt like when we'd hit a steep wave and crest it flying. You're suddenly in the air with the deck dropped from beneath you and you have to grip the wench and the rail and hang on for dear life. Like I'd be feeling myself flying sideways out over the side of the boat like some stupid kind of carnival ride. It was like hanging there when you're looking down at nothing but water under you, and all you can see is the wake churning away from the hull. Only difference was this time there's no wench and no rail to grab. So I was fuckin' flying.

"I had been just about to yell to Johnnie when he came in. Then all of a sudden I was just tryin' to get a grip on the floor. Anybody who grows up around here knows what it's like. Usually you just realize that it's over. It's like 'What was that?' And you look around for something that hangs, like a chandelier or something, and if it's swinging back and forth a little, you know you just had an earthquake. No big deal.

"But this one was like 'What the hell is --" and then "Wait! It's still going on --" and then "O fuck! Is this gonna be it?" and then "It has to stop." But it's still going on, and you think, "How the hell can it still be going on?" Then you just try to hang on and wait

215

and brace yourself. Only there was nothing I could grab. I just had to ride the floor -- the fucking floor, man."

*

The geodesic dome had sufficient structural integrity to withstand the quake, but most of the structures around it failed to some degree. The oldest buildings, mostly stone, fared the best. They had survived events such as this before, and they did so again, even though this was the most powerful quake to have hit since the city's founding. Standing amid the wreckage of so much newer construction, these older buildings seemed forlorn. They had seen their neighbors fall and be rebuilt and fall again, and they knew that it was only by the grace of some element in their original design that they had survived.

Many of the newest structures, great towers of steel and glass, remained standing, though in most cases great sheets of glass or of the wafer-thin stone with which their steel superstructures were clad, had dislodged and fallen, slicing the air with a terrifying rush of sound, as when the guillotine lever releases the heavy blade. Mid-morning, the sidewalks had been crowded with shoppers. And in the first seconds of the tremor, panicked office workers had feared that the swaying buildings would be their tombs and had run out into the open streets.

The displacement of such a great volume of the earth's crust created, while the earthquake lasted, a nauseating sound overwhelming all others. When it stopped, other sounds surfaced: an eruption of pain, screaming howls of agony wrenched from the bowels of the damned, aching groans, weeping, shouting, pleading, and maniacal laughter.

Soon after came the first explosions, as leaking gases hit broken wires or open flames. One such blast, in the Transbay Terminal, ignited the buses parked closest to it, which themselves then set off a half-mile line of them parked on the raised roadway that extended to the western anchorage of the Bay Bridge. Like a string of firecrackers lit by a giant child looking down on the Chinese New Year Parade and wanting to shock the long green-and-gold dragon dancing along Market Street, the fuel tanks burst in rapid fire, a thrill of horror. A pall of smoke quickly blanketed The City with the choking, stinking air of Hell.

*

Marty
"I felt instantly alert, as if all my previous life had

been a deep sleep from which I came now all at once fully awake, preternaturally awake. The clarity of everything I saw took my breath away. It was as if I were seeing things for the first time. And it wasn't just my eyesight: my other senses had become as acute. I could hear everything, the loudest and faintest things each defined, nothing canceling anything out. I seemed to hear where everyone around me was -- their breathing, the soft sounds of their limbs and garments shifting, even their hair moving, it seemed.

"At first I lay suddenly and still on the floor, looking at the priest's oddly voluptuous white garment, its voluminous folds mottled with the vivid hues thrown by the stained glass overhead. I knew without looking that Johnnie and Joe had come into the chapel and felt where they had been thrown to the floor. I got quickly to my feet, extended my hand to the priest and pulled him up with me.

'I heard Joe wail Siria's name behind me, and still gripping the priest's hand looked him in the eye and asked 'Where is she?'

"'Parish House,' he answered. 'Right across the street.'

'I called out to Joe and Nick. My voice sounded just as it does when I am calling to them from the foredeck, telling them how to haul on the sheets to trim the sails. I turned to look at Julie, who was already looking at me. She nodded to let me know that she was alright

and to say 'Get on with it.'

"I looked back at the priest and asked 'Which street?'

"'Ferris Place,' he said. I knew then which building it would be, a small stone structure, probably the oldest in the neighborhood, nestled up against the sheer cliff of Telegraph Hill. It must have dated from the earliest settlement of The City. It had always been one of my favorites, and I had always wondered who owned it. I admired the fact that the owner had held out against what must have been fortunes proffered by the developers of the towers that now hemmed it in.

"I heard Joe hurrying up the nave to join me and Nick at the crossing and called out the answer to his yet unspoken question. 'North!' I shouted, pointing to the door at that end of the transept. As the three of us sprinted toward the north entry, I noticed the boy of glass still lying on his side next to Julie, hugging his knees to his chest. Nick, Joe, and I hit the doors running and, throwing them open, passed into the intense white sunlight. We were blinded momentarily, and stopped in our tracks for a second until our eyes could adjust and we could get our bearings. But the scene which our eyes struggled to take in, and which our minds refused at first to understand, held us anchored where we stood.

"The Chapel was set in the middle of a great concrete plaza that formed the base of SpinWare Tower. The plaza was landscaped with raised flower-beds made of

red brick and a large jet d'eau that, remarkably, was still sending its rushing pillar of water twenty-five feet into the air. I remember its fine, cool mist blowing into my face and through my hair. Kitty-corner across the intersection at the north-west corner of the plaza stood the Parish House, at least for now. The way before us was certain, but the path seemed beyond comprehension.

"Directly across the street to the north, just to the right of the Parish House, what had once been a complex of retail shops, restaurants, and a theater, with apartments rising ten to fifteen floors above, was now a tangle of twisted steel thrusting upward from a pile of broken concrete, curled rebar, and broken glass. The dust was just beginning to settle, revealing the shapes of the ruins beneath its blanket of what seemed like fine, gray flour.

"Then I saw how many of the shapes beneath this thin, dirty snow were people, or pieces of people, sliced apart by falling sheets of glass or crushed by falling stone and steel. I vomited, and I heard Nick do the same. Only Joe had continued pressing forward, apparently seeing nothing but the Parish House toward which he half ran, half stumbled, calling for his wife.

"Then Joe seemed to trip, though there was nothing over which to trip, and for a second I thought another quake might have hit, throwing him off-stride. But then I realized that he hadn't stumbled: he had

220

slipped. I watched Joe catch himself, regain his footing, and stop for a minute.

"Most of the plaza was running with blood and strewn with entrails, and with whatever the contents of those entrails had been, whatever had been inside the panicked crowd when the great panes of glass came loose from the towers and rained down on them. I could see that Joe was beginning to take in what had caused him to slip and what, he now saw, lay all around him. Nick and I had recovered enough to be jogging carefully again and closing in on Joe, and as we got close, I could see that his face was twisted in a knot of horror and soaked with tears.

"His mouth opened and again his wailing 'Siria!' made my own guts cringe, as if my body sought to pull itself inside itself to hide from his cry. The sound seemed to rise from deep in his belly and to rip his inner being up by the roots and hurl it, howling, into the air. Joe choked and sobbed and then again his throat split wide with the howl, 'Siria! Siria! Siria! Siria!'

"Nick and I had both slowed our pace so as to keep our footing on the slick pavement. You seldom realize that ordinarily, when you are walking or running, you always look down at your feet. But Nick and I didn't dare look down We kept our eyes fixed on Joe and on the Parish House beyond.

"Then the nightmare of the real turned on us again.

We had just reached Joe when the windows on the top floor of the Parish House blew outwards, followed by a great sphere of green flame, like a child's birthday balloon attached to the nozzle of a tank of helium and filling so rapidly that the child winces, anticipating that it will burst. The insubstantial balloon of green flame had in a moment replaced the top floor of the house, and its heat burned our faces almost a full block away. Joe had begun moving again, but now he reached the curb and stopped, as if nothing survived within him that could move his body anymore.

"Nick groaned, 'No!' I tried to breathe but could not. Then, in the silence of my own suspended breath, I heard voices coming from the burning building. Cries for help went up, and in the midst of them I could hear Siria calling out to Joe.

"Joe turned to look at me, to see whether I heard it too. He could see in my eyes that I had. He smiled and stepped into the street. He got only about a third of the way across the intersection, however, before the fire's heat crippled him, and he fell to his knees.

"Nick and I knew that we had to drag him back or he would die too. If Siria was going to be saved, it would not be by any of us. He pleaded with us to let him go. If he could not save her, he wanted to die with her. He cursed us and struggled, kicking and biting and damning us for our betrayal. I thought with a shudder that perhaps I was betraying him, betraying his love and Siria's. I thought I was going to be sick

222

again.

"As I gulped air to keep my stomach down, I heard it -- him -- the boy who was made of glass -- striding toward us from the Chapel, moving with that swift grace with which he had come to us along the beach that first day, as we were leaving. I didn't have any idea what he was doing, but my chest was suddenly ready to burst with glee, the thrill of hope.

"Joe saw him too and stopped struggling in our arms. The boy of glass came right up to us but did not stop, didn't even break stride. Nick shouted 'Hey!' as he passed, but he did not respond. I reached for his arm, but he was beyond my grasp.

"The glass boy walked straight toward the Parish House. As he reached it, he lowered his head and began to run, like a bull charging a matador, he ran through the doorway.

"Joe fell sobbing to the ground, amid the mess of gore and ash. Nick went pale. Again I could not breathe.

"Then we saw the form of the glass boy emerging from the fire, and I remembered what I had thought had been a dream: this same form emerging from the monstrous surf and storm crashing all around me: the glass boy bringing my mates, my brothers, one by one to safety. I saw that this time he had two people, one under each arm. It was Siria and another woman, who wore the tattered remnants of a bright blue dress,

223

now singed and mostly torn away.

"The boy got back to the three of us but again did not slow his pace.

"'Follow me,' he said as he passed.

"We rose and followed him."

225

PART FIVE

"There is a crack, a crack in everything --
"That's how the light gets in."

Leonard Cohen, **Anthem**

Thirteen

Johnnie had been laughing as he and Joe entered the Chapel, but his laughter stopped as he looked up at the great dome under which they passed. He then cursed himself for tripping over his own feet, for looking up instead of looking where he was walking. He had fallen down in front of everybody like the Goddamn fool that he had always known, deep down, he was. Only then did he realize the fact of the earthquake.

Unwilling to trust that it was over, Johnnie lay on the ground while Joe leapt up crying out for Siria. He was only tentatively rising to his feet when Marty took charge and led Joe and Nick out the doors and toward the Parish House. As they burst out into the blinding sunshine, Johnnie was standing by himself, still half-way down the nave, and looking at Julie, who was sitting on the floor with the glass boy's head resting in her lap.

Johnnie could not stop his tears. Looking at Julie, who was speaking softly to the boy and stroking the side of his face, he remembered the sound of his own mother's voice, when, on long drives out of the city on hot summer nights, he would fall asleep on the car seat beside her, his head resting in her lap, her voice resonating through her body and into little Johnnie's ear, which was pressed against her belly, as she sang the old songs that she loved. He began to walk toward Julie and the boy, feeling profoundly alone.

When Johnnie reached Julie and the boy of glass, he stood looking over her shoulder and into the boy's face. The boy seemed to be sleeping and, in sleep, to have gone far away. The priest stood beside them, too. An older man, whom Johnnie realized must be Gus, was walking toward them.

Johnnie looked down at the glass boy. A kaleidoscope of colors played across his face, fragments of shattered sunlight. When they had first met, Johnnie had seen himself, seated in his own home, reflected in the boy's face, and he had wanted to stay close to him. Now he saw only restless shapes of light ranging from the surface to some deep interior reflected back at him, and Johnnie hunched his shoulders, shivering.

*

Gus
"When the glass boy suddenly got up and began to run out after Joe and the rest of them, Johnnie looked like he wanted to run after them too, but at that moment we all became aware of the sounds from outside. It

was as if the boy, when he threw open the doors, had let the noise in with the sunlight. I don't think any of us had really noticed what we were hearing till then: sounds that made your stomach clench, that didn't even sound like voices, really, just horrible, horrible --.

"It was the priest who seemed to really hear them, to listen, and understand. 'We have to get ready quickly,' he said. 'They will be coming in moments, if they can -- and if they cannot, we must go and gather them in.'

"'Tell me what to do,' Johnnie said.

"'Through that doorway,' said the priest, pointing behind himself, 'you will find the choir room. Bring all the robes out here, and see if you can't find some scissors in there too -- check the choirmaster's desk. We need to start cutting bandages.

"'I'm on it,' Johnnie said, running off.

"The priest then told me to go behind the altar and into the sacristy and to bring back all the communion wine I could find. As I turned to go, he looked at Julie and sent her to the kitchen for cleaning supplies, buckets, and knives. While I was finding my way around back of the altar, I saw him stepping up to it, kneeling before it, crossing himself quickly, his head bowed, before he followed Julie to the kitchen. Within minutes we were ripping all the cloth we could find, water was boiling in huge pots in the kitchen, and the

chapel was becoming a makeshift hospital for the tortured souls who soon began to pour in under the shelter of the blue-green dome."

*

William Ferris the Third had grown furious when the lights in the Press Room went out. His fury redoubled when they came back on and he saw that the boy of glass had disappeared.

"What the fuck was that all about?" Billy demanded of Louis. "And where the hell is *he*?"

Louis felt himself trembling at the tone of Billy's voice before he even heard his words. He hated his boss's anger more than any other thing about him. Even when, as now, Billy contained himself enough to speak quietly, Louis trembled. Billy's ordinary abuses, his regular exploitation of Louis, and even his arrogance, concerned Louis hardly at all compared to Billy's anger.

Louis sensed something dangerously out-of-proportion in Billy's rage, and whenever a wave of it broke over him, Louise felt his own self-control, as well as his thoughts, and even his feelings swept away. He collapsed in on himself, helpless and numb.

So Louis had learned to responded by drawing a line around Billy's rage, to establish some safe ground for himself. It was as if the tempest could be made an island, so that the sea could be calm.

"I couldn't tell what happened in the dark," Louis said, "and I didn't know myself he was gone until just now. I'll check the hallways and the rest of the floor. Maybe he was just trying to get out of the darkness himself. I'll have a look and get back to you immediately. He can't have gone far. He was probably just frightened of the dark -- he is just a boy."

"He can't be frightened of anything. I think somebody stole him. Somebody planned the whole thing," Billy replied.

"Well they couldn't get very far, if they did. I'll alert Security while I'm checking the floor in case it is just a matter of a child wandering off."

"That boy is not a child," Billy said, "or at least not the kind of child who wanders off. He doesn't take a step without a purpose. Believe me. I've seen him in action. I've been watching him for three days now."

"Yes, of course you're right. I'll make a quick

sweep and be right back. We'll find him one way or another."

As Louis slipped out through the green room, Billy turned around to present a reassuring face to the Press who were astonished to have seen a presentation by Ferris that had not unfolded with perfect precision. They were startled, and then titillated, to have witnessed William Ferris suffer not only an electrical malfunction but an emotional one as well, though the exact nature of the latter they could not as yet determine.

Billy smiled and made jocular reference to children afraid of the dark, leaning casually against the lectern and using every rhetorical and attitudinal figure he could to smooth things over. His eyes swept the room. Marty and Nick, too, were missing. Billy's right hand, which he had sunk casually into the pocket of his trousers, now clenched in a tight, hard fist, unseen. And Julie Sands was gone, too. He felt his face grow warm and knew that it reddened, try as he might to keep hidden what he was beginning to feel.

Louis returned quickly and held his clipboard out for Billy to read the notes he had jotted on it: "Not on this floor. Security watching every checkpoint, entrance, exit." As Billy glanced at the words, Louis could see that

Billy's rage was not subsiding as quickly as it usually did. It had in fact risen again, and it was about to erupt.

His own shaking frightened Louis. He was terrified to feel himself thrown up against a wall, and bewildered to realize that he had not been thrown by the enraged Billy Ferris. In the time it took him to understand that an earthquake was in progress, Louis fell to the floor, and he saw Billy likewise thrown to the ground. A tripod supporting a television camera toppled over on his boss, the heavy camera falling directly on Billy's head.

Louis struggled against the heaving floor to make his way to his fallen boss. The tremor stopped as he reached Billy. Carefully, Louis lifted and rolled the camera off of him. Blood ran down Billy's face from a long gash that began in the middle of his forehead and extended across his left eye, slicing to the middle of Billy's cheek.

Louis was crying as he pulled off his shirt and tore a large piece of it away to press over Billy's wound. Holding it firmly in place with one hand, he used his other hand and his teeth to continue ripping the shirt into long strips with which to tie the bandage in place. He wondered how he could tell when the time came that he could risk relieving any of the pressure with which he was now staunching the flow of blood in order to tie it in place. He saw that Billy's chest was rising and falling, but the great man showed no sign of consciousness. Louis could feel the tower swaying, and he found himself trying to keep track of the passing time by counting its movements, like a metronome. Slowly, it came to rest.

As Billy began to come around, he struggled, flailing his arms and arching his back, even kicking a little, trying to push Louis away. But the devoted assistant resisted and stayed on top of Billy until he became fully conscious and at last lay still. Opening his right eye, Billy looked up at Louis and quietly said, "Sorry."

Louis took a deep breath, saying nothing, but he worried whether the blow might have caused some brain injury to his boss. "Sorry" didn't make any sense in this context. After all, "sorry", in Billy's lexicon, was a synonym for "bad" -- more polite than "piss-poor" but otherwise the two were interchangeable; as in, "that's a sorry excuse for a quarterly report" or "global research is in a sorry state these days". For a moment Louis thought that perhaps his own appearance prompted the remark, that he might be looking disheveled and even dirty to his awakening boss.

Then to Louis's amazement, Billy added, "I'm sorry. I'm so sorry."

Louis tensed up again. Stopping the bleeding was simple enough, but what would he do if Billy weren't in his right mind? How could he handle both his boss and the situation around them? The extent of the disaster had begun to become apparent to him, and Louis knew that they, he and Billy, must respond to the emergency immediately.

Billy's eyes now focused on the bloody shirt Louis had momentarily lifted from his face, and then he looked back at Louis.

"Thank you," Billy said. "Thank you."

Louis faltered for only a moment. He quickly straightened himself and said, "Sir, you have --"

"No," Billy said. "Billy."

Louis took a breath and began again. "Mr. Ferris. We have to start getting these people down the staircases." He gestured with his head to the rest of the room, where the men and women of the press were beginning to right themselves and to try, tentatively, to stand, checking themselves for injury and wary of the very ground beneath their feet. "This building can withstand any number of tremors and aftershocks, but not fire."

"Not fire," Billy repeated softly, his eyes closing slowly as he spoke. "Not fire."

"Mr. Ferris," Louis said firmly. "Mr. Ferris. We have to get everyone out of this building in case of fire."

"Not fire," Billy said again, under his breath. Then, to Louis's great relief, Billy's right eye became clear, his gaze steadied, and he grabbed Louis's bloody shirt in his own hand, pressing it against his left eye and allowing Louis to tie it in place.

"Louis," Billy said, as he began slowly to get to his feet, "you lead these folks to the north stairwell. I will take care of directing anyone else on this floor. O -- and ask a couple of them to hold back and help us organize this thing."

Louis grinned. "Yes, Mr. Ferris," he said, standing up and reaching his hand out to steady Billy where he stood.

"Thank you, Louis," Billy said.

"You're welcome, Sir," answered Louis.

237

Billy looked out with his one good eye at the frightened reporters picking themselves up off the ground. "If you'll excuse me," he said in the confident voice that they had all so missed during the press conference, "Louis here will lead you out. I have to see to the evacuation of the rest of the building. We will have to finish our presentation later. Thank you all for coming -- and safe home."

*

Billy Ferris had known that in an emergency such as this, cell phones would fail. Those few transmission towers that might survive the earthquake would be jammed by the overwhelming number of calls being dialed. He had therefore seen to it that SpinWare Tower had an internal communications system, with its own secure fiber-optic lines and back-up power generation, that could function even in situations such as this. So, after circling the floor to make sure that everyone was proceeding to the stairwells and down to safety, Billy stood at the red emergency phone box near the elevators, making calls to his lieutenants throughout the building.

Had any part of the building failed? Was anyone likely trapped? Any missing? Were any of the evacuation routes blocked or otherwise compromised?

All the while he was making these calls, Billy was staring at the pane of glass in the small door on the iron phone box that he had opened. The little door had swung open and stood parallel to the dark paneled wall behind it. As he talked, Billy watched the reflection of his own battered face in that small pane of glass.

Whatever pride William Ferris the Third suffered under in his daily life, his understanding of his current purpose and his confidence in his own competence were honest and true. Through it all, however, he could not stop wondering what had happened to the boy who was made of glass. Where had he gone? Where?

*

Gus
"Julie, Johnnie, and I were helping the priest, Pappas, with the first aid supplies at the center of the crossing when the North Door banged open, and the glass boy came striding in supporting Siria and another woman, one under each arm. The women could barely stumble toward us. They were smeared with soot and coughing as though their lungs were trying to come up.

"Marty and Nick and Joe were right behind them. Joe shuffled along. I worried that he might be injured. Then I saw the clots of blood and ropes of gore covering his shoes. He was simply trying not to slip and fall while catching up to his wife and the boy of glass. I took hold of Siria to help her stand, and Pappas did the same for the other woman. The glass boy let go of them and then even he stumbled, as if about to fall in a heap himself.

"'Reverend Pappas,' the woman said as she slumped in his arms. 'Father --.' She tried to speak but her chest heaved with coughing and sobbing.

"'There, there, my child,' Pappas said, holding her in his arms and gently stroking her dark hair. 'All shall be well. Shhh. Shhh.'

"Joe had reached us now and took Siria in his arms. She too was sobbing.

"'What happened?' Julie asked, looking at Marty and Nick. 'Where did you find them?"

"The other woman answered, looking at Pappas as she spoke. 'I'm so sorry, Father. There was nothing we could do. Everything is gone.'

"Pappas looked at her as if she spoke in a foreign tongue. 'Gone?' he asked.

"'Looked like a gas line or something,' Nick cut in.

'Whole top floor blew in one great ball of fire.'

'Pappas's face went white. He looked into the eyes of the woman in his arms. 'Father Verre?' he asked.

"She began sobbing again, nodding her head, and opening her mouth only to choke on words she could not speak. Pappas crossed himself and held her closely. 'There. There, my child,' he said, tears flowing down his face. 'All shall be well. All shall be well. All manner of thing shall be well.'

"Pappas helped the woman lower herself gently to the floor, so that she could sit with her back against a glass wall for support. When he stood upright again, all expression had gone from his face, leaving a blank -- like a death-mask out of which his clear eyes stared at a lost world. He began ripping choir robes into long strips for bandages.

"Joe helped Siria to sit, too, and sat beside her, holding both of her hands in his. She leaned against him, resting her head on his shoulder, and then suddenly laughed. She took one of Joe's hands and pressed it to her belly.

"'He's kicking!' Joe shouted. 'He's OK! He's kicking!'

"None of the rest of us had any idea until then that Siria was pregnant. We all laughed, even while we were still crying, and crowded around the pair. The *woman smiled and wept afresh. She looked up into Pappas's face, which I saw was now alive again. 'The Lord giveth --' he said."*

*

"All accounted for," Billy said to Louis as they regrouped after a long hour overseeing the evacuation. They were standing in the midst of the cavernous lobby on the ground floor, and the lines of evacuees flowing past them had begun to thin. "All but one, that is," he added in a quieter voice. "Have you heard anything?"

"Nothing," Louis said as they joined one of the lines toward the main entryway.

"He has to be here," Billy said, "but none of these people have seen him, or we'd know it. I just don't --"

Billy's sentence broke off as they reached the great doors to the SpinWare Tower and saw for the first time the pandemonium outside: the devastation, the lost crowds, the blood, the dead. The sun had climbed high overhead, and the day was growing hot. Yet it was getting darker, too, the sunlight taking on a greenish cast as it fought through the plumes of smoke rising thick, black, and heavy above them and stretching behind them to the horizon. Day was fast becoming night, and still it grew hotter.

Billy hesitated just inside the doors, as if he wanted to stay inside his Tower regardless of the danger, but Louis said "Look!", pointing toward the Chapel of Saint Nicholas. Long lines of people, walking singly or bunched in twos or threes, were making their way to the Chapel and going inside.

"Of course," Billy said. "Of course he would go there."

They broke into a trot but were slowed, as Joe had been, by the mess that covered the ground everywhere. They were coughing from the gathering smoke, too, and their eyes were stinging by the time they finally got inside, under the dome.

Involuntarily, both men raised their eyes to the vision of Christ above them as they entered, and when Billy lowered his, he stopped for a moment, like someone who has entered a room and realizes that he has forgotten why he is there, forgotten what it was he had come to find.

Fourteen

Nick

"Heading back to the church, I realized that it was getting really dark, almost like really late afternoon or even after sunset, even though it was still late morning. I looked up and saw the smoke rising from downtown and spreading out over the rest of the city, like some big highway overpass getting wider and wider as it stretched back across the sky. Then it was like my body felt all disoriented: it was getting darker, and it was getting hotter. Both at the same time. That never happens. If the sun is going down, everything is supposed to cool off. Your body expects it and can't deal with it being darker and hotter at the same time. It felt like we were in some kind of other world.

"It had gotten so dark that the streetlights started coming on, at least some of them. I guess they were the ones that were still getting electricity, and the smoke blotting out the sun made their sensors think it was night. It was weird, really weird.

"Then when we had done everything we could at the church, we'd used up all the cloth we could find for bandages, washed the wounds we could with wine for the alcohol, and let people who were hurt the worst even drink some for their pain, we all finally left the church. I don't know what the hell time it was. I mean, there hadn't been much we could do anyway. We probably only really helped the ones who were

pretty well off to begin with, if we could stop their bleeding and bind them up.

"But using the wine to sterilize wounds or help some of the pain -- that was probably just pissing in the wind anyway. And it almost fuckin' made me cry the way the people kept thanking us and blessing us and telling us that they would remember us in their prayers for the rest of their lives -- like there would be much "rest of their lives" to begin with. Man, I had to just nod and literally bite my lip and keep going with what I was doing.

"The people who were really bad off, outside, the ones stuck under parts of buildings or cars or I don't know what -- or wounded like you couldn't imagine -- they sometimes screamed so loud you couldn't think. You wanted just to go find them and shut them up for good, since that seemed to be what they wanted. Then they'd stop and you'd wonder if they were dead or just gave up but lay there still in all that pain. Sometimes you'd hear one of them pleading with a cop or a soldier who happened to walk by to shoot them, beg the poor guy to shoot them right there. And sometimes you heard a shot.

"There were already tons of cops and soldiers swarming through the streets. I wondered where the hell they had all come from. It was like all along there must have been a secret little world underground that none of us ever heard about, full of cops and soldiers -- like under Disneyland there's all those underground

245

streets and offices and passageways for Dopey and Goofy and the cops to pop up anywhere without warning.

"We were actually lucky to be in a kind of out-of-the-way little corner, almost like a small bay or cove of the city. The SpinWare Tower was nestled in almost up against the cliffs of Telegraph Hill, which meant solid protection all along the west side, and it was surrounded by this huge plaza of brickwork and fountains and lawns, all of which made a kind of firebreak, and we were in the middle of it.

"The few buildings on the far side of the street, when they did start to burn, they just weren't enough of a critical mass for the fire to jump across all the pavement and brickwork, and the winds that might have pushed the fire over were diverted north and south by the cliffs behind us and the hill, which created wind-tunnels bending everything to either the north or the south. There were just a couple of old buildings -- like the Parish House -- on our side of things, and they burned up pretty quick and then died out.

"So the fire would have had to spread along the Embarcadero to ever get to us, and they were hitting it with everything they had all along the waterfront, from the fireboats on the bay. They turned their hoses on the piers and on everything they could reach, as far inland as they could shoot the water. I guess we might have even been able to stay there except that we had run out of everything we had to try to help people, and *everyone who could move was getting out as fast as they could anyway. Only the ones who weren't ever gonna make it out of there were left.*

"We -- I mean Johnnie and me -- we wanted to get across town and out to the valley and back home, but looking at that ton of smoke spreading everywhere, I knew we were screwed. All downtown was on fire. You could see it. I was about to give up. I figured I'd be OK if I hung with the glass boy. He already saved me once, and he'd just saved Siria and that other lady. But Johnnie was determined to make it home.

"Johnnie kept saying he could get us through Chinatown. I was, like, 'O yeah, man, right: the whole fucking place is blazing away.' But a little later I saw Johnnie and Joe talking off to one side, and Joe was nodding and nodding like he agreed with everything Johnnie was saying.

"I guess Joe had heard that there were these tunnels under Chinatown, a huge maze of them, and so he bought it when Johnnie brought up the tunnels and said that he had not only heard of them but knew his way around the whole neighborhood down there. Johnnie said he could lead us all past the fire by going under Chinatown. Then we'd be home free.

"Joe was pretty much desperate to get Siria -- which meant the baby too, of course -- home. Siria herself seemed to be asking Johnnie all kinds of questions and looking pretty skeptical. I figured she might want to

247

stick close to the guy who'd just saved her too. She would glance over at the glass boy from time to time, I noticed. But he wasn't looking in her direction and didn't see.

"In fact, the glass boy was standing off a bit by himself, except for Gus came up to him after a while and they seemed to talk a little bit. Marty and Julie were talking by themselves, too, but then they went over to Gus and the glass boy and all four of them looked like they were making plans. That was when I knew that we were all going to go our separate ways and I began missing him already.

"I guess I wouldn't have minded hanging around with all of us still together for a while, but you could already see the creeps mingling in with the crowds of people who were walking up and down the waterfront trying to figure out how they could get on any kind of boat that could get them across the bay. Usually creeps like that don't even come out in daylight. They stick to shadows, doorways and alleys and stuff.

"Then again, like I said, it was already getting dark, or maybe things were getting too hot for them where they were -- OK, bad joke, I know -- but anyway, these creeps were working themselves in among the regular people who were all distracted and afraid and looked totally lost anyway. I could see the scum would be grabbing whatever they could as soon as they could. They'd start by ripping off the weaker ones, but pretty soon they'd be getting bolder and nobody would be safe.

"It was all only gonna get worse -- a lot worse -- and so all of a sudden we were all saying goodbye to each other -- which I hate. I started to try to say something to the glass boy and almost lost it. All I could say was 'See ya, buddy.' How fucking lame is that?

"I shook his hand. It freaked me out how cold it was even with the heat all around us. Then I had to turn away. I started walking very slow toward Chinatown, figuring that Johnnie and Joe and Siria would catch up. I kept my head down like I was thinking, but every now and then I glanced back over my shoulder at them.

"I felt like everything in the world had fallen apart. For the first time in my life it seemed like maybe there wasn't gonna be a future, like there wasn't anything to hope for anymore. And I felt like I'd spent all this time with him, and I hadn't learned anything at all. I was too fucking stupid to have asked him questions and really gotten to know him or at least something from him. It was kind of like I'd been there, but I'd missed everything, you know? If that makes any sense."

*

Reverend Pappas had left the Chapel of St. Nicholas only after every bit of food and drink, from the contents of the church kitchen to the communion wine, even the

Host, was gone. He left only after every clean scrap of cloth that could be found had been used to bind a wound and the bins of clothing collected in the annual drive for the homeless had been wrapped around the ones in need. Today the whole of The City had been made homeless, the just and the unjust, thief, beggar, poor man and rich man, all. But even so, they were the lucky ones. Many had suffered far worse, including Father Verre.

Reverend Pappas prepared to leave, first genuflecting before the altar and then turning to face the empty, domed space he so loved. He stood in the pulpit, the place from which he used to look out over the congregation of the faithful, the place from which he had had the temerity to preach the Word. The thickening smoke had so obscured the sun that the light attempting to pierce the pall overhead was failing more and more minute by minute. What light did manage to find the stained glass of the dome shone only darkly, making the watery heavens richer and deeper than Pappas had ever seen.

Reverend Pappas stared into the great curve of the ocean that poured down in front of him. The light by which he saw came now more and more from the flames outside, and it agitated the algae and the manatee, petrel and porpoise, shark and anemone, which all wavered, shimmering, in the flowing water. Hearing himself take a deep breath and hearing his heart sounding rapidly in his ear, Pappas felt his legs holding his weight and thankfully felt his soles relaxed pressing against the ground.

His composure regained, Reverend Pappas saw that the point in his field of vision on which he had been focused for some time now was the image of the Risen Christ, exalted in Heaven, walking on water. Today, in this light, the great dome melted, dissolving itself into water, under the feet of the Lord. Tears running down his face, Reverend Pappas made his way down from the pulpit, along the nave to the East Door, and out into the great square at the foot of the SpinWare Tower.

He saw waves of people ebbing and flowing along the Embarcadero. He heard the tumult of their voices: rage and denunciation, weeping and shrieks of pain, commands barked and supplications cried out. Himself now homeless, the priest walked slowly toward the mass of humanity churning along the waterfront. He remembered the beauty of the old Parish House, the beauty of the morning light falling through the window in his bedroom and across his little writing table: all now ashes, and home now to the ashes of

251

Verre, his dear friend.

Reverend Pappas walked slowly toward the crowd. As he did, a figure hurried out from the shadows around the base of the SpinWare Tower to join him. The priest noticed the man only when he had caught up with Pappas and put his arm around the priest's shoulder. It was Louis, and the two of them merged into the flowing crowd and disappeared together.

*

Marty

"It made perfect sense to me that Nick and Joe wanted to get home as soon as possible, if their homes were still there, to save them or to salvage what they could from them, but I still didn't want to let them go. I could see no sense in staying in The City at all. There would be nothing but trouble, with so many thousands stranded out of doors, homeless and hungry and destitute.

"And it would be hell trying to get any kind of aid, food or clothing or tents or any medical supplies or anything, either across the bay or all the way around it, with both the freeways collapsed and the railroads all twisted and broken. Even if you managed to get all the ferries and barges and various pleasure craft to help move supplies across the water, who the hell was going to manage and direct all that traffic? How

many could make landing at any given time? How much room was there at the piers on either side? How could you load and unload with the kind of pandemonium that was going on all up and down the waterfront. And in any case, wouldn't it be better to be on the other side, where everything that might eventually make it over here would have to come first?

"I had to just let go of any desire help them and let them go where they would. I said goodbye to Nick and to Joe and Siria -- and to Johnnie too -- and then set out with Julie to follow Gus and the glass boy to Gus's boat in the marina, where he lived. We were going to have to hike all along the great curve of the Embarcadero, out past Fisherman's wharf. We'd be taking our chances, too, if the fire spread to North Beach too quickly.

"We set out along the narrow waterfront that wraps around the foot of Telegraph Hill. The fireboats had been doing a great job and had prevented the fire spreading toward North Beach that way. It still might have come up through Chinatown, but there was a stiff wind out of the north and east, created by the immense heat of the fire which rose rapidly and sucked the air in from across the bay. These winds then fanned the blaze, pushing it west along the Market Street corridor. Sooner or later it would reach the marina, but with luck we'd be out on the water by then.

"As we made our way around Telegraph Hill, we

could see the crowds of people coming down every street, coming together along Lombard, the wide boulevard becoming a human river flowing toward the open spaces of the Presidio. I watched people coming down the slopes of Russian Hill, wearing backpacks, carrying suitcases and ice chests, as if going no further than to a car at the curb, preparing for a picnic or camping trip. I saw an old Asian woman wheeling, with great effort, an old-fashioned sewing machine, one of those powered by a foot pedal rather than an electric motor. At first I thought the poor thing must be out of her mind, but later, when we passed Chrissy Field and I saw people trying to rig up makeshift tents out of sheets and blankets and towels, it occurred to me that a woman with a sewing machine could probably make a lot of money in the coming days.

"People had their dogs and cats with them too, some on leashes and some in crates that they carried along. I was surprised by the number who walked along with colorful exotic birds, parrots and macaws and other kinds I couldn't name, riding on their shoulders or their arms, like they were cartoon pirates. Others had canaries and parakeets in elaborate birdcages. A few walked solemnly with big snakes, four or five or six feet long, wrapped around their upper bodies.

"As we went along, I noticed how people reacted when they saw the glass boy. Nearly all fell silent as he passed, some bowing their heads or making the sign of the cross. I wondered what they saw when they looked at him, and what they thought.

"Most surprising of all, this huge crowd of old and young, rich and poor, black, white, Latino, Asian, gay, straight -- all had the air of people going to a concert or fair or embarking on a picnic. Neighbors who had never seen or spoken to one another were chattering away, even laughing aloud, telling intimate truths about their lives or entertaining with jokes and anecdotes, while children chased each other around them, weaving in and out of the knots of adults proceeding down the streets. Young men and women stopped beside the aged, who were sitting on bus-stop benches or leaning against parked cars to catch their breath. The young half-carried the old ones, who leaned on their shoulders, and they shared their bottled water with the thirsty and their Powerbars with the faint.

"We made it to the marina and got into Gus's boat. I pushed us out of the slip and away from the pier, hopped on board, and helped raise the sails. We had to fight the strong north wind that the fire was sucking in off the bay, tacking back and forth for over an hour before we got out into the channel and caught the incoming tide and another wind, this one coming in off the Pacific, blowing through the Golden Gate and heading east, with us. Once our sails caught her, we made good speed.

"As we did, I realized how calm I had felt and was feeling in the midst of this disaster. In fact, I felt not only calm but relieved. It struck me how hard I had

been working to bring old Billy down, when, with a
shrug of a shoulder, or maybe the batting away of an
irritating fly that troubled her sleep, life -- the world --
had devastated him, along with all the trifling works,
the vain grandeurs, of which men -- and women -- are
so proud. I might have saved myself the trouble, I
thought.

"And then I thought of poor old Billy when I last saw
him, standing in that chapel, looking kind of dazed by
it all. I actually felt sorry for him: the guy had lost
everything that mattered to him in a few seconds. I
thought how lucky I was to have had relatively little --
nothing really, at least in Billy's terms -- to lose. I
wondered how -- and whether -- he'd ever get over it."

Fifteen

Johnnie did not like to say how it was that he knew his way around the tunnels under Chinatown. He let on that he had, as a little kid, tagged along with a Chinese friend from school who showed him how to get quickly from the schoolyard to some of the interesting places downtown, knowledge which could make a kid some money, not to mention set him free from many a boring recess or study hall. But the fact was that Johnnie had learned to navigate these tunnels from his father.

From the time that Johnnie was five, his father would grab him by the hand and take him along when he went to collect bills. Johnnie never forgot the first time his father took him along on collections in Chinatown. They entered a restaurant and, ignoring the hostess who greeted them as they came through the door, his father made a hard left turn and trotted down a steep staircase to the restrooms and kitchen below. Little Johnnie hurried to keep up with him.

They walked down the narrow corridor, the air redolent with the odors of old cooking oil, sour milk, and ageing meat, and passed the door to the kitchen where Johnnie saw something bloody, something big and bloody, being hoisted onto a high table. They continued past the restrooms, too. At the end of the corridor stood a door marked "No Admittance," which Johnnie's father opened, holding it open with one hand and reaching back for Johnnie with the other.

His father took hold of Johnnie's shoulder as he stepped through the doorway and pulled the boy along with him into a place so dark that Johnnie could not tell whether it was a closet or hall. The door swung shut behind them, and the blackness was absolute.

Little Johnnie had felt a moment of panic as the dark closed in on his chest and the room squeezed the breath out of him. He could not inhale: the darkness had expanded and forced all the air out of the room. It pressed against the boy from all sides. Inside, Johnnie was screaming silently, but fear of his father kept even the slightest sound from escaping. After what seemed many minutes, Johnnie's eyes adjusted to the darkness, and he realized that he could see the long, narrow, low-ceilinged room which they had entered.

Even at the age of five, Johnnie knew that his eyes had adjusted to the dark more quickly than his father's and knew to take advantage of that fact. He had time to study the place, to look for corners or doorways or open passageways that might serve should he need to escape. He would always be prepared. This room, however, disappointed him, for it looked to be a dead-end.

A single, narrow aisle ran the length of the room, crowded on both sides by shelving on which Johnnie had expected to see restaurant supplies. His father, now able to negotiate their way though the dark room, began to lead him down the aisle toward the far end. As they passed, the boy shuddered to see that each shelf along the way held the body of a man. He remembered the bloody thing on the table upstairs and felt sick. Then, however, Johnnie saw that these men were breathing, though they remained silent and motionless otherwise.

"Poor devils," his father muttered as they passed row after row of bunks.

Johnnie wanted to ask what was going on and who these men were, but he felt his father's grip on his shoulder tighten so hard that the boy squirmed under it as they walked. His father's fingers dug in under his clavicle, and Johnnie struggled to avoid crying out.

"Don't you ever fucking get mixed up with this shit," his father hissed under his breath.

"Opium has the devil in it, and once he's got his nails into you, he'll never let go."

They had reached the far end of the room, where Johnnie could finally see that it was not a dead-end but had another entrance. This was clearly the main entrance, he now saw, and they had come in through the back door. A much larger and more ornate door stood at this end of the room, and just inside it, a wizened old man sat on a high stool behind a podium of sorts, a strange parody of the hostess they had passed in the restaurant upstairs.

The old man greeted Johnnie's father in a whisper, and in whispers they haggled. Johnnie already understood these formalities, and he knew that in the end the old Chinese would pay Johnnie's father what Johnnie's father said he was owed. Everyone did, eventually. They all knew the consequences of not paying off Johnnie's old man, who brought his son along not only to appeal to their sympathy for a man who had small children to support but also to remind them of their own children and of their need for protection.

As Johnnie's father was at last receiving his payment, the ornate door swung inward, and two young men, also Chinese, came in laughing and talking to one another with the boisterousness of drunks. They froze the moment they saw two round-eyes, a man and a boy, looking at them. They were about to turn and run, but the old man waved his hand, and they stood to one side of the door, trying, it seemed, to squeeze themselves into the shadows and disappear.

"Come on, son," Johnnie's father said, pulling him by the shoulder and thrusting him ahead through the wide doorway and into what the boy now saw was a tunnel leading off into the darkness of the earth.

So it was that Johnnie's education in the system of tunnels under Chinatown began. In the ensuing years Johnnie's father took him through the maze of corridors making his collections hundreds of times. Now, leading Nick and Joe and Siria into this underworld, Johnnie smiled to think that for the first time in his life, he had reason to be thankful that his father had been the man who he was.

*

Gus
"I had noticed the glass boy standing where he had stopped when he had first returned with the women. He had not moved a muscle. I remembered how he had stood alone that first night on the trail, after he

261

had entered into the fire. He was somewhere within himself, I knew, pondering something, fathoming some depth only he could know. I let him alone a while, as long as I could, then approached him and asked as gently as I could whether he was OK.

"'My father,' he had said. I stayed silent, having no idea where he was going. 'My father,' he said again, 'was in that building.' Everything drained out of me instantly. I felt numb.

"'You mean,' I asked, 'he is gone too? Like Father Verre?'

"'No no no,' the glass boy answered. 'Not that way. I mean that he -- that in the -- my father was in the fire.'

"The chill that went down my spine physically shook me. All of a sudden I felt afraid of the glass boy. The love I had felt was gone in an instant, and I drew back, skeptical and wary. I wondered how far in over our heads we might all be.

"From then on I kept a close eye on him. While we all did what we could to help the wounded in the Chapel, I was alarmed to see how easily everyone else accepted the glass boy as part of their familiar world, as I had done. I felt as if the scales had fallen from my eyes and I was watching everyone else going on wrapped in the shadowy fog of ignorance which I had shaken off.

262

"I had become used to thinking of the boy who was made of glass as a slightly different kind of human being. Now I realized how easily my assumptions had kept me from strict observation. Looking at him I no longer saw that young boy who seemed to be heading somewhere, on a quest of some kind. Instead I was asking myself what kind of thing this was that stood before me. I found myself watching him from somewhere deep inside, someplace untouchable by anyone else.

"I always say that I am enough of a skeptic to believe in things I cannot know. My mind is, after all, human. I admit the reality of the invisible as well as the visible. I'm not even sure there's much difference.

"You don't have to have spent any time at sea to imagine, for a moment, the ocean, arching away from you in every direction, wrapping the planet. Think of the horizon on that ocean, the line where water gives way to sky. Think of that vast curved line along three-quarters of the globe, and you are already wrong. There is no line.

"All across that vast surface, molecules of water stand up in rows, poking up like fence-posts, and molecules of air are wedged down between. Molecules of water are constantly moving up, rising from their rows, and drifting into the air, while molecules of air sink into the water. What seems to be the skin of the world is not there. What is there is a region of flux and

change.

"There is no borderline between sea and sky. We see one and not the other, but what we see is defined by our nature as much as by whatever is out there. And I don't think we just make the borderline: I think we are the borderline. We see water, and we do not see air. That's the only line there is between the sea and the sky.

"I have a left and a right, an up and a down, a north and a south, but Creation does not. There is no edge where sea and sky press one against the other. Nor is there a line between me and the air or the water or anything else, really. Nothing ends at my fingertips.

"But where did the boy who was made of glass fit in this universal flux? Was he a God? Or some chthonic daemon? What was he looking for, really? And what was happening to me -- if anything. Had something happened to the world? What in fact was the world? Was it still the same world that I had always lived in? Was I dreaming? Or was the world that I always thought I'd lived in itself a dream from which I was now awakening?

"Because he had a familiar shape and spoke in recognizable words, I had taken for granted that this creature was much like me. Now instead I remembered the feeling of being in a truly foreign land -- foreign enough that sewage ran in open ditches down the streets, where the stench of unrefrigerated slabs of

meat hanging in the summer heat of the open-air market nauseated me -- and seeing a merchant smiling at me. In the first instant I took his wide grin as a sign of welcome, but then I realized that I did not know what a smile might mean there. Perhaps there a smile was more akin to the baring of a hyena's teeth, something more like a menacing growl than like a gentle kind of laughter.

"So it was with the glass boy as we hiked on around Telegraph Hill and Russian Hill and on toward the marina. I was on alert, something in me drawn taut and ready for action if the glass boy should make any untoward moves. It was only when we boarded the boat and made our way out into the bay that I could finally let down my guard a bit and take in the scene all round us.

"The smoke had been blocking out the sun for most of the afternoon, and only now as the sun sank below the plume, its rays shooting in from the western horizon, could I really see the extent of the devastation. The City that I had known all my life was simply gone, erased from the earth. I tried to remember what had stood where, and I felt ashamed that I could recall only one or two details of the skyline that I had thought I loved so much.

"I could remember some of the landmarks that had given that skyline its famous individuality: the Great Pyramid, the graceful, old-fashioned Ferry building, the iconic little tower atop Telegraph Hill built in

imitation of a fire-hose nozzle, and the elegant SpinWare Tower itself. I could not, however, fill in the blanks. The great majority of the structures that had made up The City were as lost to my memory as they were to the burning shoreline that so rapidly receded behind us.

"I remember too that as the sun set, the great black plume overhead began to glow along its western edge, where it stretched out over the sea. It glowed with an unearthly green at first, the green of yellow sunlight mixing with the filthy gray of smoke. The weird green light suffused everything, including the surface of the bay and our little craft. Marty and Julie looked sickly in that light, as I am sure I looked to them. Only the boy of glass seemed unchanged by the light, as if his flesh was not subject to the same corruptions as our own.

"Gradually the sickly green turned to a dull orange, which itself then resolved into deeper, more somber reds: magenta, cardamom, vermillion, crimson, blood. We sailed under the changing light to the other side of the bay among a flotilla of crafts large and small, until we could take our place at the pier in Berkeley.

"Having set Marty and Julie ashore, I set a course for the mouth of the Napa River. The vast conflagration of The City, reflected back by the smoke and high fog that formed a ceiling above us, revealed the earth and her waters as if by moonlight. I was able to sail up past Mare Island and Knight Island and Russ Island,

all by the light of that holocaust.

"As the sun rose the next morning, I could hear a new sound coming from The City: huge explosions of dynamite as they blew up buildings in the fire's path, attempting to create a break that the fire could not jump. I did not know it at the time, but some of the thunderous blasts were the result of further tremors in the earth causing power stations and fuel-storage tanks to explode.

"When we reached Napa, I set the boy ashore on his own and then set sail to return to The City. I had not been able to shake from my mind the image of Billy Ferris standing alone in the great square at the base of his monumental Tower, looking small and lost as we walked away from him there. I wanted to find him, whether I could do anything to help him or not.

"As I sailed out into the open bay again, grief welled up in me. I had fought off sadness until now but was at last overwhelmed. I remembered when the glass boy had been our savior, whom we followed happily on the long trek home. I remembered when he had been a vulnerable young boy full of wonder and enthusiasm, whom I had wanted to protect. I remembered his beauty and his selflessness in saving all of us from the sea and in saving the two women from the fire. I regretted the doubts that had made me treat him coldly at the end, and I wished for a return to the time when we first crested Twin Peaks and saw The City spread out at our feet, shining. I wished the return of a time

when we could hope and we could dream."

*

The boy who was made of glass had stood in the Chapel of St. Nicholas, in the midst of the people's thankful devotion, their tears of loss and of joy, and their clamorous exclamations, alone. Their chatter and noise reminded him of the bestial sound of the voices that had called to him that night that seemed so long ago, the voices that had called him out from his mother's house and into the storm. He did not concentrate enough to hear what they said. His mind was too busy to listen.

The boy of glass was beginning to understand, and his understanding dashed the naïve hope with which he had begun his journey. He knew now that his father had nothing to do with this city or these people. He understood now that his father was something much higher and far greater than they, so much greater that these men and women would have meant nothing to him. His father would hardly have perceived them and would not care about them at all if he had.

This understanding made the glass boy proud of his heritage but also sentimental about the destinies of his little friends. He regretted, too, the loss of his childish longing for his father to "come home", to be reunited with the boy and with his mother. The knew now that the journey ahead of him would be harder than he had ever dreamed possible. Its difficulty frightened him. He knew that it might very well prove impossible.

He came ashore in Napa at about 10:00 am and began hiking along the river toward the head of the valley beyond which rose the slopes of Mt. Konocti. He was following the same dry smell on the air that had led him away from the sea and toward The City those few short days ago. He hiked forty miles that day, and as the last of the sun's light failed, he had advanced as far as a mile up the lower slope of the mountain. He reached the ruins of a little house where a famous writer had once lived.

He decided to stay the night there rather than risk the unfamiliar trail in the dark of night. The cabin was so like his mother's cave -- like his home -- that the shimmering beads of glass that were his tears rolled down the sides of his face as he lay on his back waiting for sleep. He tried every trick he could think of to get himself to fall asleep, but it was only later, when a wind came through the soft boughs of the pine trees towering above the roof into which he stared, a breeze that stirred the boughs with a hush like that of the waves of a calm sea rushing up the long strand and sinking into the sand, that he slept. He slept cradled in the sound or in the memory of the sound of the watery hush of waves along the shore of a peaceful sea.

*

Billy

"I alone did not escape. I watched the others depart, going to their homes, their futures. Nick's friend Johnnie led Siria, Joe, and Nick south into Chinatown and under Chinatown to their homes in the valley, which remained untouched by the fires. Gus led Marty and Julie Sands and the boy who was made of glass north toward the marina, to the boat he kept moored there, on which he lived and in which he would carry them across the bay to safety.

"It was Gus, the only one out of all of them, who looked back at me as they left. I saw the question in his eyes and shook my head slowly in answer. I turned and walked back into the Chapel of St. Nicholas, my beautiful jewel box, the one offering I had made in my life, backhanded though that offering had been.

"When I reached its center, I sat down on the floor. I looked at the tables near the organ loft, the tables at which everyone had been so busy making bandages. They were strewn with bits of thread and lint and with cardboard cylinders empty of the tape that had

encircled them. As I looked around at the rest of the sanctuary, I saw that Julie had left her notebook on the floor where she had knelt beside the glass boy, and I saw the organist's chair overturned on the platform above. Then I looked up and saw the sunlight itself falling. I could see the shafts of light as they were made visible in the smoke and the flecks of dust that hung in the air, shafts of light falling in myriad colors, colors that it had always held within it, colors into which it was now split by the stained glass of the dome above.

"I took a long look at the creatures of the ocean portrayed in the glass all around me. I saw the most astonishing thing: as the smoke and fog outside the chapel disturbed the falling sunlight, and the sunlight from above began to mix with light from below, the light of the fires outside, firelight leaping and dancing, casting swirls of shifting shadow on the dome and the glass walls beneath it, the whirlpools and eddies of light made everything pictured in the stained glass seem to come alive. The kelp and sea-grasses swayed. The fish and eels, the rays and dolphins and whales, all swam above and around me. And the figure of Christ above me also seemed to move, walking on the water.

"I sat there feeling emptied of everything, at rest. I could think of nothing that mattered anymore, nothing that could draw me away from this place, nothing I had to do. I saw the chapel's beauty, really saw it, I think, for the first time. As much as I had schemed over its creation, and as much as I had prided myself

*in showing it off when it had been completed, I had
never simply seen it for what it was.*

*"All of that rich, glowing, brilliant glass -- I loved it.
I loved it. And not because it was my creation or my
property, but simply because it was, I loved it. For
once I sat unwatched, unseen, idle, and surrounded by
something good and beautiful and true.*

*"So when the second great aftershock hit The City,
and the dome shattered above me, I felt neither fear
nor regret nor pain. In fact, in the instant it
happened, I knew what it was, and I looked up to see
the wondrous event: the sea itself came apart and
rained down on the one who sat on its bed. As the
shards of glass pierced my eyes, I was filled with light,
the pure white light in which all colors are joined, from
which all colors come.*

*"And emerging from within that light I saw at last the
one who had been following me all along, in the clock
repair shop, in my office, and in the tower. He
extended his hand to me as he approached, and I took
it in mine. I had come home."*

*

When the boy awoke, the sun had already
climbed above the horizon, and the trail
leading up the mountainside was clear and
easy to follow. By mid-morning, the boy who
was made of glass reached a plateau that

opened out as a wide meadow that extended like an epaulette along the shoulder of the mountain. Walking out to the edge of the meadow, the glass boy saw before him the great expanse of the valleys and the foothills below, which extended to the shimmering waters of the bay, on which the sunlight sparkled and danced, beyond which the landscape disappeared into a vast dark smudge of smoke and wind-borne ash and soot. Somewhere out there his mother awaited his return to their little bay, something for which he too had begun to long in earnest.

As the glass boy was about to turn and resume his climb, he thought he heard, or seemed to feel more than hear, a rumbling sound so low in pitch that it was as if the earth had released an ancient, heavy subterranean sigh, as if the earth itself had moaned. The air became pungent again with that dry smell, tinged this time with a sulfurous edge that stung his nostrils. His father was close, he knew.

The boy of glass hiked on, and by the time he reached the summit of the mountain, he knew that his father sensed his approach. The day had grown hot, not with the warmth of the sun only, but with another heat that rose from the ground beneath his feet as the glass boy walked. Strong winds had been rising all around him in the late afternoon, hot air swirling about the mountain as he climbed the slope. In the final hour, it was a wonder to the glass boy that the forests around him had not burst into flame from the heat.

At the summit, the boy who was made of glass found a huge lake that was such a deep blue that it looked as if a piece of the clear sky had cooled and fallen into the great crater that was Mt. Konocti. Wisps of steam were beginning to rise all along the edge of the lake, white wisps that blew back and forth like long, airy scarves of the sheerest fabric tossed up and drawn through the air by invisible ballerinas dancing across the water. Going to the edge of the lake, the glass boy stood and peered down through the gathering swirls of steam into the heart of the cold blue water.

He watched a long time before he saw it, a movement, the beginning of a gleam, the light of a fire rising underwater, and he recognized his father's face. The pyroclastic dome rising within the lake was filling the ancient crater and would soon force the entire lake to spill over the rim and flow down into the valleys below. Then the glass boy saw, still far below the surface, the spreading dome rupture and spill a fire of liquid rock, boiling the lake and sending her waters tumbling down the mountainside, a lahore of steam and mud flaring into flame. The valley flooded, and then the entire mountain exploded.

The boy of glass was smiling then, as the fire and the flood lifted him, as if swept up into his father's arms, and bore him out across the foothills and down into the valleys and up over the further ranges of hills, hurling him, at last, in a thousand thousand pieces, into the sea.

*

At home, his mother heard the volcano explode. Then the shattering earthquake threw her to the ground. The point of land which included her little bay tore away from the rest of the continent and shot northward dozens of miles. When the glass boy's mother, still prone on the ground, lifted her head to look toward the distant mountain, she recognized her husband.

She knew that her son had found him, and she remained where she lay, in tears. As the tide came in, the waves lapped at her prostrate form, and still she remained, unable to move.

She lay there by the water weeping, motionless, on into the night and through the night. She wept without relief, without comfort, endlessly. She lay there another day and night, and another after that, and her grief grew.

Her sadness stretched out from her, as if it were reaching for her lost boy of glass, stretching north and south along the edge of the sea, seeking the shattered pieces of him that glinted in the sunlight, suspended in the waves and sinking under the waves. As she endlessly sought him, she felt her own life running out of her, like the wash of water behind a wave that, when the wave has expired high up the beach, sinks slowly into the shining sand.

She became her sadness, and still her sadness grew, until it, and she, encompassed all the oceans of the world, lying in complete passivity at the edge of the land, the waves breaking on her body, on her grief. She lies there to this day, dry and broken, but sparkling with splintered bits of sunlight, as if spangled with tiny bits of glass.

Go down to the sea, my friend, and stand where she lies. Listen to the waves.

Made in the USA
Charleston, SC
09 August 2010